INHERITANCE OF DECEPTION

A Benjamin Berkshire Series-Book One

Charles C Hood

Copyright © 2025 by Charles C Hood

All rights reserved.

No part of this book may be reproduced in any form or by any electronic or mechanical means, including information storage and retrieval systems, without written permission from the author, except for the use of brief quotations in a book review.

In memory of Vernia and Shirin Hood

CHAPTER ONE

Ben Berkshire entered his local grocery store to get some milk. It's not a big store, and he felt very comfortable shopping there because he knew a few of the employees and was knowledgeable of the general layout of the aisles.

He was in the dairy aisle when suddenly from behind him, there was a loud scream.

A lady was apparently having a very difficult time with her young daughter. The daughter was about 3 or 4 and was sitting in the child seat of the shopping cart. The child was kicking and starting to scream herself, seemingly out of control; but not crying, just upset about wanting or not wanting something.

The lady had apparently reached the end of her rope and started screaming herself, demanding that the child stop whining and behave. The mother grabbed the child by the arm and was shaking her; not viciously, just trying to get her attention.

As he watched the apparent out-of-control scene, he wondered how a hostile relationship like this between a mother and a child could develop.

Sure, all families, at one time or the other, will have some disagreements and acting out is a common way for it to be expressed. However, in a grocery store, most mothers with a daughter or son at that age seem to be more pleasant and in control. The experience usually appears to be a happy one with laughter and talk.

Then, he got his answer. Around the corner came a man. He looked to be a few years older than the mother, maybe 35, six feet or so tall, a nice tan and a haircut that says he is most likely in the business world. Ben assumed that the two adults were educated and married.

The man was not happy. He ignored the child and spoke to the mother (his apparent wife) in a harsh, angry tone. "How long are you going to be in here, Patricia? I can't wait all day! I have to get to the office for an important meeting. You know that; but you seem not to care. And now you are in here shopping and having a fight with Michelle over God knows what! She should be in preschool by now. Have you no sense of time?"

"Well, you should have picked up my car from the garage yesterday." With tears welling up in her eyes, she added, "And if you had not started that fight at home this morning, I wouldn't be such an emotional wreck! Why did you have to bring up such a subject the first thing in the morning, Henry? Why can't we have a normal "good morning" and some coffee, before you jump into our personal lives? Just get out of here and go to your precious office and girlfriend. Michelle and I can get home without you!"

Henry paused, took a good look at Patricia and then at Michelle, then went over to his daughter still sitting in the shopping cart and gave her a kiss and a hug, and said, "Daddy loves you, sweetheart." Then he turned around and left the store.

For some reason, Ben felt some pain about Patricia's situation. Her tears became uncontrollably strong. It wasn't that he wanted to take sides in their fight—he just felt the need to console her.

He walked over to her and offered his handkerchief. She looked up at him in a bit of surprise, paused, and then took the handkerchief. She wiped her eyes, and said, "Thank you."

He did not reply, just smiled. After a moment or so, he said, "I hope I'm not intruding, but I couldn't help but hear your conversation. I'm sorry for your problems. May I offer you and your daughter a ride home?"

"Oh no! I wouldn't want you to go out of your way. We can call a cab; we don't live far from here."

"But, really, I don't mind, and I too live in the neighborhood." He reached out his hand and introduced himself, "I'm Ben, Ben Berkshire, I live over on Cias Trail."

She took his hand and said," Patricia Morgan. We live on Dennison Drive."

Ben nodded and said, "Yes, I know where that is. So, it's settled. I'll get you and your daughter safely home, after you have finished shopping. I'm in no hurry, so go about your business, and I'll be close by when you're ready to leave."

"I only have a few more things to pick up and we will be ready."

Ben waited at the store entrance for them to check out and then helped Patricia take her groceries to his Toyota Highlander, which had plenty of room in the back for her groceries.

As Patricia watched, Ben lifted Michelle out of the shopping card and opened the back door for her to get in. She hesitated, so he reached out and took her hand and introduced himself. She shook his hand lightly then got into the car. Patricia placed her safety belt around her and closed the door.

Ben placed her groceries in the back and closed the hatch door; then opened the passenger door for her to get in.

Ben tried to have some small talk with Patricia on the way, but she was still deeply in thought. He asked her what her address was, and she said, "Oh! I'm sorry—we're at 1423 Dennison Drive."

"No problem. I know where Dennison is—just off of Hanna, right?"

"Yes."

They rode in silence the two miles from the store, so they were there in a few minutes. He pulled into her driveway and stopped the car.

"Here we are!" Ben got out and opened Patricia's door so she could help Michelle out of the back seat. Then he opened the rear hatch to get Patricia's groceries, and helped her take them into the house.

It was a two-story, stone and wood home. Relatively new, maybe three or four years old, with white trim; beautiful flowers in the front and lining the walkway from the street. It looked like a real home, a place where people took pride in its appearance.

After they put the groceries on the center counter in the kitchen, she said, "I can't tell you how much this means to me—to be rescued, and I really appreciate the ride home, so thank you!"

"It was my pleasure. I hope everything works out the way you want it to." He started walking to the front door, but turned around and handed Patricia his business card. "If you ever need to talk, or need help, just call. I'm no more than a mile or so from you."

She took the card, looked at it, and said, "Thanks!"

He left the house and started for home. Then, realized that he had not picked up the milk! So he went back to the store, bought the milk, and headed home again.

But his thoughts were on Patricia. She seemed so sweet and kind. And her heart was broken because of a situation that appeared to be not of her making. She was tall, maybe five foot five with shoulder-length, curly red hair. She appeared to be between 28 and 30 years old; seemed to take good care of her health and looked to be in good physical condition. How could her husband be unfaithful?

When he got home, his little sidekick, Tula, was waiting, tail wagging and very happy to see him. Tula was a 17-year-old black-and-white Shih Tzu. She had no teeth, was deaf, and blind in one eye. Sounds terrible, but she was in very good physical condition. She walks at least a mile with Ben almost every day, and can jump up onto the bed and couch. She is very happy, and Ben was always super kind and easygoing with her.

Tula was his late wife's dog. Barbara had passed away almost four years ago, after over 17 years of marriage. It is impossible to explain just how painful it was to get over her passing.

For over a year and a half he really wasn't sure that he would survive. But, thanks to a wonderful grief group at the local church, he was able to come to terms with the loss and establish a new life without her.

CHAPTER TWO

"Really! You are a masseur?" Patricia asked.

"No!" Ben said, "I give full, pleasurable body rubs."

"So, what's the difference?"

"Well," he gave her a sideward pleasant smile, "a masseur is concerned with your physical fitness and muscle tone, and a body rub is focused on the natural body pleasures and enjoyment."

"How on earth did you get involved in such an unusual talent?"

"Oh, it was something that I picked up while visiting Hong Kong many years ago. I met a lady at a restaurant called the Silver Dollar, a wonderful steakhouse! Her name was Lee.

"We had a few drinks and dinner and she invited me back to her place. While there, I noticed that she had a separate small room off the living room and I could see a massage table through the open door.

"During our conversation, I asked her if she was a masseuse. She explained the difference to me and gave me a book to read about the art of pleasurable body rubs. The title was *Awakening the Natural Pleasures of the Body and Mind*.

"I still have that little book somewhere. It provides the detailed history of the pleasurable body rub, dating back over a thousand years. It also gives you detailed instructions on how to give a full pleasurable body rub."

"Did Lee give you a body rub?" Patricia playfully asked.

"Well," Ben said with a smile, "yes, she did. And it was one of the most amazing, erotic experiences that I've ever had."

"Really!"

"Yes!"

The front door opened and Patricia's husband, Henry, burst in. "What the hell are you doing in my house?" he said gruffly to Ben.

"I'm a neighbor, I live just up the street. I'm Ben, Ben Berkshire."

Henry settled down somewhat and said, "And why are you here?"

"I was returning your wife's scarf that she left in my car the other day, when I gave her and your daughter a ride home from the grocery store." He turned to Patricia and said, "Well, Ms. Morgan, you have a nice day."

"You too, Mr. Berkshire, and thank you again for the ride and for bringing my scarf to me."

"You are very welcome."

Ben looked at Henry and said, "I didn't get your name."

"Henry, Henry Morgan."

"It was nice meeting you, Henry." Ben turned and left the house.

"Why the hell didn't you tell me that a man gave you a ride home?" Henry said to Patricia, in a loud, angry voice.

"Why would I? You showed no concern for how we were going to get home. You were too busy worrying about getting to your office! And, now, all of a sudden, you have concerns? No, I think you are just afraid that some other man is showing me some attention. If you were half as nice as Mr. Berkshire, I would not have been stranded at the store in the first place.

"It has been very difficult for me for the last few weeks, since you told me about *her*. You seem to think that just because you admitted to the affair, it's now ok and that we should just begin resuming our normal lives.

"Well, I can't do that, Henry! I can't pretend that nothing has happened. You see her every day at work and you want me to 'get over it'? WELL, I CAN'T AND I WON'T!"

Patricia turned and left the kitchen, went up to the bedroom, and slammed the door behind her. She leaned her back against the door.

She could still feel the warmth from Ben's flirtation. He was so soft spoken and seemed to be such a kind soul. Tears came to her eyes as her thoughts drifted to her husband's infidelity and his obvious lack of love for her.

She longed for a loving relationship again. But it seemed that they were just not going to make it together. Divorce had always been a dirty word in her family; but she could not live the rest of her life with someone that did not respect and love her.

CHAPTER THREE

"Try to keep your head still, as you go through the ball," Ben said to his friend Helen. They were at the golf course and he was giving her a lesson on putting.

Helen is a fair golfer, but just can't seem to stay in position when completing the putting swing, if the putt is over three feet long. As she gets about halfway, with the putter almost at the ball, she tends to turn her right knee inward and swing her right hip around. Such a move causes her putter to go across the ball and off its target line.

"I don't know what I'm gonna do with you, sweetie! After almost two years you still insist on swinging that hip," Helen laughed and said, "Maybe you need to hold it in place."

He smiled. "Your mind just can't stay focused."

"You have that effect on me, Ben, I can't help it!" she teased. "Maybe it's time you paid me some attention. You haven't been over for several months. I could cook some salmon, open a bottle of wine and, who knows where it might take us."

Ben gave her a hip bump, smiled, and said, "Oh, I know where it would take us, lady! Let me take a rain check for now. But I won't forget the offer."

"Alright then, but don't wait too long! I'm a busy gal you know."

"I know."

Helen started to go to the club house and Ben started practicing his putting. He was leaning over to putt when someone beeped their horn just behind him. It was loud, and he jumped a little as he looked around.

It was Patricia Morgan. She waved with a full grinning smile and drove into the nearby parking lot.

Ben waved, then returned to his putting.

Helen stopped and said, "So I have some competition! Who is that classy lady?"

Ben shared a bit of information on how they had met. Helen laughed and said, "So!"

Ben laughed too. "No, not really. Patricia is a married woman in my neighborhood and I have had no involvement with her."

They both headed over to the 19th hole for a beer and to relax. It was around 4:00 p.m., and after an hour or so, Helen left to meet a friend and Ben started going to his car. His habit was to walk through the pro shop as a shortcut to the parking lot, always looking for a different hat or glove.

Rounding the hat rack, he saw Patricia looking at some shorts. He walked up behind her and said slightly loud, "BEEP!"

She turned around, startled, with a beautiful smile and said, "Hey, you!"

"Hi."

They talked a while about the clothes and hats and laughed freely. It was a good visit, though short.

"Well, I best be getting home to feed my dog."

"Would you like to drop by later and have a glass of wine?" Patricia asked him.

Ben hesitated then said, "That would be great, but I didn't feel much warmth from your husband when I met him."

"Well, we separated the day after you were at the house and he moved out. Nothing to do with you—just some serious personal issues that cannot be resolved. I will be filing for divorce soon."

"I'm sorry to hear that."

"Anyway, Henry is in Chicago on business, so you don't have to worry about his bad manners; because he won't be coming by."

"Well, if you think it's ok, I would love to."

"Of course! It's fine. How about eight?"

"Eight is good."

They said goodbyes and he went to the parking lot and got into his car.

Ben's mind was going a thousand miles an hour on the way home. Patricia is such a warm and exciting person. And today she seems very happy.

When he got home, Tula was jumping around, tail wagging a hundred miles a minute. He leaned down and kissed her on the head. She was ready for something to eat and needed to take a walk.

While opening her food, he let her out into the backyard to take care of her business. She is so good! Never wanders off or follows any other animals away from the house.

He put her food into her bowl and she started barking, telling him that she wanted in. He opened the door and she went straight for the food. He always gave her soft food because she had no teeth—and she still ate like a champ!

After she finished eating, she found the walking harness and leash and waited for Ben to put it on her, knowing that they were heading for the park, which is about one-half mile from the house. There and back is all she could handle.

She ran loose at the park with a couple of other small dogs for about 15 or 20 minutes, and around 7:00 p.m., he hooked her up again and they went back to the house.

When they got home, he decided to give her a bath, as it was Tuesday, one of her normal days for a bath. She is small and very cooperative. The shower is large, with large showerheads on three sides, and a seat running completely across the short side. It's a great shower!

Anyway, Tula just walks into the shower with him. She doesn't mind being bathed at all. She is so small that he can hold her in one hand and shampoo her with the other; then he just lays her in a cradled position on her back on his arm and

shampoos her underside. It only takes five minutes or so. When they were finished and Ben dressed, it was 7:45 p.m., so he started driving to Patricia's house.

On the way, he decided to stop at the specialty wine market and grab a bottle of red wine. He picked up a bottle of Rodney Strong Reserve Cabernet Sauvignon. Yeah, he knew it was expensive, but hey! He didn't know where this might go! LOL!

He arrived just on time, rang the doorbell, and when the door opened, he was so surprised that his mouth fell open for a second or two.

Patricia had on a light-green silk dress that clung to her body. She was stunning! And very sexy! Her beautiful red hair was pulled back into a large ponytail and her face and hazel eyes radiated joy.

"I'm the TV repairman, were you expecting me?" he joked. She laughed and put her hands on his arm.

"Well, NO! But if my date doesn't arrive soon, you have a date!"

Ben kissed her on the cheek and said, "You look absolutely ravishing! And what a beautiful dress!"

"Well, thank you, kind sir! Come in! Come in!"

As they closed the door, he showed her the wine and asked her if she wanted it cool or room temperature. She said room would be fine. She looked at the bottle and commented that he shouldn't have bought such an expensive one.

They went into the kitchen and he asked where her little girl was. Patricia said that she was spending the night with her sister-in-law and brother-in-law. They have a young daughter just three months older than Michelle.

"How old is Michelle?"

"She's three and a half, going on 10," she said with a laugh.

Patricia had made a mixed salad, and put some cheese and crackers in a small bowl.

Ben opened the wine and poured each of them a nice serving. She touched her glass to his and said, "To a new friendship." He smiled and said, "I feel that it's already underway." She smiled and laughed slightly.

They were leaning against the counter across from each other, maybe two feet apart. They both tasted the wine, and nodded approval to each other.

The conversation became quiet and Ben asked, "Is everything ok.?"

"No, not really. I'm afraid I'm not very good company. I have spent all day trying to make a decision about my future after this marriage. As you heard, Henry is involved with someone at his office, and has been for over a year. It has really crushed me. We used to love each other so much. Now we are separated, with no intimacy in our lives, and heading for a divorce."

She started to cry. He pulled her closer to him and held her lightly, hoping to provide some comfort. She put her arm around him.

Then the doorbell rang!

She moved away from him, smoothed her dress, paused, and went to the door. Her sister-in-law, JoAnn, was at the door with Michelle.

"I'm sorry to interrupt your dinner, but Michelle had a fall. Not a bad one, but she insisted on coming home."

"Of course!" She asked JoAnn to come in. Ben introduced himself and offered her a glass of wine. Michelle was fine and went straight to the living room to watch TV.

Patricia, JoAnn, and Ben had a glass of wine. It was obvious that JoAnn wasn't leaving soon, so Ben told Patricia that he had better get home and check on his dog. She looked at him with a disappointing glance.

He took her hand and kissed her on the cheek. Ben told JoAnn that it was very nice meeting her and said, "I'll let myself out."

"Thanks for dropping by, and thanks for the wine."

"You bet." He left the house.

Ben was frustrated because he obviously could not provide much advice or comfort to Patricia. Her marriage problem was something that she would have to work out with her husband.

After Ben left, JoAnn was excited about him being there. She looked at Patricia and said, "What the hell! Who was that gorgeous man? And where did you find him?"

"Oh, he's the guy that I told you about that gave Michelle and me a ride home from the grocery store after I had that blowout with Henry. He's just a neighbor."

"Bullshit! We've known each other forever and I know how you think and act."

"That knock'em dead dress and your makeup, with wine—and when I came in, it looked like you had been rolling in the hay!"

Patricia laughed with the woman she had known since college at William and Mary. They were close friends and both had taken pre-law there.

With many dates and drinking parties together, they were very close. And, they married brothers. JoAnn married Arthur, Henry's younger brother. And they all wound up in Atlanta.

"Well, he was so damn nice and sweet about giving me a ride home that day. He even called to check on me—with sincere concern. Then just the other day I ran into him at the country club, and I just automatically invited him over for a glass of wine." Patricia smiled and said, "I mean, you know, Henry has moved out and, so what the hell! I just wanted to get to know him a bit."

"Sure," JoAnn laughed, and said, "and you just happened to put on your sexiest hot dress, just to get to know him a bit? Oh, my, you are one lucky girl! It looks like I came just in time to save you from God knows what—or, I spoiled the most wonderful time you might have had in many months."

"Well, it wasn't meant to be either."

They both laughed and had some more of the expensive wine and talked about days of old at W&M.

Patricia had already shared with JoAnn the problems that she and Henry were having and that he was screwing around with his Personal Assistant, Bridget Monet.

Actually, JoAnn was aware of that before Patricia told her, because Arthur had mentioned that it might be the case. JoAnn wasn't even sure about Arthur's faithfulness, but didn't have any tangible proof otherwise.

"So, what are you going to do?"

"Well, obviously, Henry and I will be getting a divorce. I will have to evaluate everything and try to make a decision about my future. What that might be, I'm not sure. But I can tell you for sure that I don't plan to stop seeing Ben. Not yet, anyway. I just have to get to know him better to be able to tell for sure," She smiled a big smile, "He does know how to get the juices flowing. I had already passed the point of no return when you rang the doorbell."

"What a guy! Well, you deserve some excitement and happiness in your life, after all that Henry has been and is putting you through. That bastard!"

CHAPTER FOUR

Ben arrived home, and Tula was excited to see him. They had a few minutes together and then he went to the kitchen and poured brandy to sip on while he did a computer search for Henry Morgan. He thought, *I just wasn't satisfied with his demeanor.*

He pulled out the keyboard from under the desktop and turned on the iMac computer. First, he checked Google for Henry Morgan living on Dennison Drive. A bio immediately popped up.

Henry Morgan, age 36,

married to Patricia Hampton Morgan, age 31.

CEO and Owner of Morgan Development Inc.,

a Real Estate investment brokerage company; primarily investing in apartments.

Headquarters in Atlanta, Georgia. 3200 Peachtree Ave,

Six employees:

Vice President of Operations, Arthur Morgan (his younger brother),

Director of Investor Coordination (Jesus De Angelo),

Sales Representatives, Julie Desoto and Lonnie Weinstein,

Personal Assistant, Bridget Monet.

Secretary, Martha Blitz.

Current Assets 35 million dollars.

So, it appeared that Henry was a high roller with lots of daily pressure. Might explain his attitude toward me, but to his wife? He didn't know. There just had to be more to it than just a bad-hair-day syndrome.

And while Patricia and Ben had not discussed him, it was apparent that she wasn't happy at home. But still, he wasn't sure that it was wise for him to interject himself into such a disrupted relationship. It just didn't feel like a good idea with her still married.

It took a lot of processing, but Ben finally decided that it would be best if he didn't get intimately involved with Patricia at this time. He had to figure out a way to explain that to her without hurting her.

The following morning, Ben texted Patricia and asked her if she would like to have some coffee. She immediately replied, "My place or yours?" Ben said, "Well, I'm at the "Brothers" coffee shop just across the street from the grocery store, just swing by here."

She hesitated, and replied "Sure, no problem."

Twenty minutes later Ben saw her drive up in her beautiful apple-red Mercedes hardtop convertible and park in front of the coffee shop.

When she entered the shop, a couple of guys sitting at the counter locked in on her beautiful smile and very defined body. She was wearing a pair of light-blue, not-too-tight pair of shorts and a fitted, soft white top. She was just gorgeous! With a body all men dream of!

She came over and slid into the booth across from him. He gave her a big smile and shook his head. "You make a helluva entrance, beautiful lady!"

She laughed a little and said, "So, does that mean that I haven't been rejected?"

"No! You have not!"

"How do you like your coffee? I'll get it from the counter."

"With a little cream, please."

He slid out of the booth and ordered her coffee, which came immediately. Returning to the booth, he bent over to her and kissed her on the cheek.

"Thank you!"

"It was all my pleasure!"

They took a couple of sips of coffee and then she said, "Look, I'm pretty good at reading people and situations and I sense that we are not on the same page that we were on last night. Is that true?"

"Wow! You do like to get to the bottom line."

"Well, yes."

"Look, last night was the most wonderful and exciting night that I've had since my wife passed away. You made me feel that I was worthy of having a new life with someone else. I loved the idea of a relationship with you."

"But?"

"But, as much as I would love to become involved with you, my intra-self and moral compass is causing me some major guilt issues. I feel that it just isn't right for me to interfere in your life and marriage at this point. If you were separated for a longer time or divorced, I would grab you up and never let go.

"Just in this brief time that I have known you, I'm well aware that you are a kind, loving, and devoted mother. You obviously have a great deal of love and happiness to share with someone that deserves it. And, I feel that your husband doesn't deserve you. But you *are* married."

"Well, I know that you are no lawyer! You seem afraid to quit talking. Ben, I understand how you feel and I deeply respect your position. I guess I was lonely and, yes, excited about you entering my life, because, even though we live in the same house and sleep in the same bed, Henry isn't there anymore. And hasn't intimately touched me for at least a year.

"He abandoned me for someone else; his personal assistant in his office. They have been involved for at least several months and it doesn't appear that it is over." Tears started rolling from her hazel eyes. "It hurts me deeply."

He handed her a napkin and held her hand. "I'm so sorry, Patricia, you certainly deserve better."

She didn't say anything for several minutes. Then she said, "I too, understand that what almost happened last night was not a good idea. "But," she said with a slight smile, "you were so damn nice, I just couldn't stop thinking about what could have been."

"Me too! And I don't want to stop seeing you. Matter of fact, I refuse not to see you in the future. You need a loving friend and I'm your guy! Ok? I will be available to help you, to talk and text with you, and hug and kiss you as a loving friend, for now.

"And, if there is a time in the future when it's appropriate for us to extend that friendship to a closer relationship, we'll be ready.

"But, if you decide to get your marriage back on track and can make a go of it, then, maybe we can still be friends. How does that sound?"

She started crying, and he moved over to her side of the booth and held her in his arms and softly kissed her on the forehead and cheek.

After she regained her composure, she looked at him and smiled. "You are a gorgeous, loving, and very sweet guy. And I love you for that. I want very much for us to continue our friendship.

"But," she said, with a big healthy smile "I won't be wearing that green dress again anytime soon!"

"Please don't! I don't think that my will power is that strong. You looked too delicious in it!" Both laughed.

They left the coffee shop around 2:00 p.m. as he needed to check on Tula and his mail at the post office.

On the way, he rehashed their conversation and felt that it was the most reasonable way to respect Patricia's marriage and, at the same time, stay in touch to provide her support. Whatever that might be.

Soon he had to travel out west for a couple of weeks on business. But he planned to maintain contact with Patricia. He felt comfortable with their newly established relationship.

CHAPTER FIVE

After eight years with the Texas Department of Public Safety (DPS) where he worked as a criminal investigative attorney, he felt that he needed a change. He and his wife, Barbara, had lived in the Austin, Texas, area for 10 years. After her death from breast cancer, he tried to continue his life there, but too many things reminded him of her.

After a year or so following his wife's death, he decided to relocate and start a new life. He liked the Atlanta area and he had enough business contacts there to get his new business going. So he left the Texas job, moved to Atlanta, and opened a private investigation company, Investigating Services, Inc., in College Park, just outside Atlanta.

His friends and neighbors were always trying to introduce him to their female friends. But Ben was a long way from wanting to get involved with anyone else. He just wanted to stay busy and let time help him survive.

His Investigating Services Company specialized in white-collar crime cases. His primary clients were state Attorneys General and their staffs. With his background in Law Enforcement and as an attorney, he was well equipped to assist in tracking and evaluating an individual's involvement in white-collar crimes. Plus, he made an outstanding expert witness.

On Sunday, Ben had to pack for a trip to Phoenix. The following day, he had a meeting scheduled at 10:00 a.m. with the Assistant Attorney General of Arizona, Mr. Martin Perez, whose office is in the State Capitol Building on Washington Street.

Ben arrived in Phoenix at 9:05 a.m., got a cab to his hotel, the Hyatt Regency, Downtown, checked in, and had his bag sent to his room, #411. Then he went to the bar and ordered a cup of coffee.

His hotel was just a short distance from the Capitol building and he had some time to kill. He wanted to review some correspondence that he had received from Mr. Perez regarding the case.

The case appeared to be pretty straightforward. Some folks have set up a front company or companies to launder money being obtained from the sale of Mexican heroin.

Small aircrafts are being used to bring the heroin into the U.S., primarily into the Prescott Valley area just northwest of Phoenix, then shipped out by trucks to Las Vegas, NV, and Los Angeles, CA, areas for distribution.

The front company is a real estate investment company, "Transport Reality," located in Phoenix.

Ben arrived at Mr. Perez's office a few minutes before ten and introduced himself to a lovely young lady at the reception desk, Juanita Cruz. Juanita appeared to be in her mid-20's, with dark hair and had the most pleasant smile that showed both in her lips and her eyes. Beautiful!

"Please have a seat and I'll tell Mr. Perez you are here."

Shortly, Mr. Perez came out and said, with a smile, "Sorry to keep you waiting, Mr. Berkshire; it's a typical Monday morning."

"No problem," Ben said and presented his hand. "I'm Ben."

"Yes, and please call me Martin."

"Nice to meet you, Martin."

"You too, Ben."

"Care for some coffee?"

"No thanks."

They sat down and Ben removed his notes from his briefcase. "I looked over the material that you sent me. It looks like they have a thriving business."

"Yeah, in the past year we're estimating over 100 million dollars going through this area alone."

"Do you have anyone on the inside yet?"

"No, we wanted to gather more information and financial data before proceeding. That's the reason we wanted to bring someone into the case that isn't local or regional."

"Who else is on the team so far?"

"We have a few guys in finance, and one international drug unit member."

"No locals?"

"No, we haven't vetted them yet. We just can't take any chances on blowing this one."

"That makes sense. Ok, Martin, what role do you want me to play?"

"I was thinking that maybe with your DPS and investigative experience, you could first meet with our financial people and see if there are any clues as to where the money is coming from and going to. Right now, we just can't seem to connect the dots."

"That sounds good. Just point me in the right direction, and I'll get started."

"Great! I'll text you the names and where you can meet. How long will you be in Phoenix?"

"I was planning on a couple of weeks, initially. Does that seem reasonable to you?"

"Yeah, that's good. Once you make contact with my people, you can keep in contact through emails and then come back here as needed. Does that work for you?"

"You bet. I'll leave you to it, and after I receive the names of your financial contacts, I'll set up a meeting with them and we can get to work."

They walked to the door. "I really appreciate meeting you, Ben, and look forward to working with you."

"Same here, Martin."

As Ben passed by the receptionist area he glanced over at the desk and Juanita was watching him with that big friendly smile. He smiled at her and said, "Thanks for your help."

"My pleasure!"

Ben returned to his hotel for some lunch and to check out his room.

He settled in at the café in the hotel and had a shrimp salad, half of an egg salad sandwich, and a nice cold beer.

As he reviewed the correspondence from Mr. Perez in greater detail, he realized that there were several companies already identified as possible money-laundering organizations.

Transport Reality has direct connections with a couple of other companies—"Multiple Family Investing" in Seattle, WA, and "Title One" in Chicago, IL. So, it looked like there would be a lot of files to work through before he could get a true understanding of the operation.

He went to his room and walked across the spacious room, passed the king size bed, and went onto a very nice corner balcony. The sun had passed overhead, so the balcony was somewhat shaded, and the view of the city was very nice!

He called to the front desk for info on restaurants. Leticia answered with that golden friendly voice, "Front Desk, this is Leticia, how may I help you, Mr. Berkshire?"

"Hi, Leticia, I was wondering if you could direct me to a good Mexican restaurant. I'm from Texas and would love to find some great fajitas."

"Blanco's is a 5-star restaurant and has fantastic Mexican food. Plus, they are known for their frozen margaritas. It's on Washington, not far from our hotel."

"Sounds great! Thanks for your help!"

"My pleasure, Mr. Berkshire."

He got a quick shower and changed clothes and went downstairs to get a cab to Blanco's. It was around 8:00 p.m., and there was a waiting line for dinner, so he signed in and settled onto a barstool and ordered a beer.

About halfway through his beer, he noticed a woman at the check-in area having a heated discussion with the hostess. She was about 30-35, long dark hair, nicely dressed, and very pretty. He stepped closer and realized that the discussion was about missed reservations. She had apparently made the reservations a while back and was waiting for her party of two more.

He stepped over and said, "Excuse me, but I heard your conversation. I have a reservation and you're welcome to it. I don't mind waiting for an hour or so at the bar."

"Are you Ben?" asked the hostess.

"Yes."

"Well sir, your table is ready right now."

He looked at the lady and said, "I'm Ben, Ben Berkshire; please take it. I'm alone and really not in a hurry."

She looked at Ben then at the hostess and said, "That's so nice of you, but we can go somewhere else."

"But," Ben said, "I understand that the food is outstanding here!"

"Yes, that's what our hotel told us."

He smiled and said, "So, eat, drink, and be merry!"

She laughed "Ok! Under one condition—you must join us! I'm Lois, Lois Harding. I have two of my girlfriends meeting me. We are visiting here from Boston."

"Ok! I accept, but I get to buy the first round of drinks."

She smiled and said, "Deal!"

The hostess looked very relieved and happy to have the problem resolved without losing any of her customers. She said, "Please follow me," and led them to the table where Ben and Lois were seated.

Ben noticed that Lois was well groomed, expensively dressed in a blue silk dress, and she was wearing a beautiful gold Cartier watch. This was not your typical visitor in town.

The waiter came and Ben asked Lois, "Should we wait for your friends before ordering drinks?"

"No, we can order for them. They will be along shortly and we all love frozen margaritas." So Ben ordered four frozen margaritas.

"What brings you to Phoenix, Ben?"

"Work, I'm afraid. I have business here and will most likely be here for a couple of weeks."

"What kind of business are you in?"

"I'm a private investigator and work with state governments on white-collar crimes. Mostly boring research stuff. And because it is with government entities, it's all very security conscious. How about you? What brings you so far from home?"

"We are all three fashion designers and have a private company in New York. It's called The Chic Basement. We're attending a private showing of some wonderful clothes. The designers are from Hong Kong and Tokyo. But they are very western thinking in their designs."

"Where is this showing?"

"The Hyatt Regency on Washington."

Ben, smiled and said, "What a small world, that's where I'm staying."

They had a good laugh when she said, "We're staying there also!"

After about 10 minutes, Lois received a text from one of her friends and they had decided to eat somewhere else. So, it was just this beautiful woman and Ben. He smiled to himself!

"Looks like you're stuck with me. But I would understand if you would like to leave."

He smiled. "I wouldn't dare leave a beautiful lady by herself in a strange town with all these *men* running around on the prowl."

She laughed and said, "My hero!"

"You bet! I'm in it for the long haul."

"Ok, then, but I get to buy the dinner."

"Deal! Now, let's get started on these other two margaritas!"

Lois and Ben spend over two hours at Blanco's, laughing and talking about anything and everything. She was such a delight. Her family was old Boston but she went to NYU for her education.

Her daddy didn't like that too much because the family assumed she would attend Harvard, where he and all before him had gone.

Lois was obviously cut from an original cloth and decided that New York was best for her and what she wanted to do; and that was to design her own clothing line.

The waiter came over and advised them that the restaurant would be closing at 11:00 p.m., and that was only 20 minutes away.

They laughed as Lois paid the bill. She asked the waiter to call a cab and said to Ben with a laugh, "Darling, are you ready to go home?"

Ben laughed and said, "Yes, my dear."

It was a short ride and Ben paid the cab driver as they departed. He asked her what room she was in.

"520."

"Well then, I'll walk you home, to make sure you're safe!"

She smiled. "You are so kind, sir!"

They took the elevator to the fifth floor, Ben walked her to 520, and she opened the door.

He kissed her lightly on the cheek and said, "Good night, my dear lady. It was a pleasure spending the evening with you."

"Thank you, kind sir. I enjoyed it too. Good night."

She paused and Ben said, "I'm in 411, if you need anything."

"Thanks! Good night, Ben."

"Good night, Lois."

After Ben left, Lois decided that she wasn't quite ready to turn in, so she went down to the bar to hook up with her friends.

CHAPTER SIX

Ben got up early, opened the shades to let the morning in, ordered coffee from room service, took a shower, and shaved. He had an email from Martin, providing a couple of names for him to contact.

One was from the finance group, a Ms. Florence Becker. Florence works in the banking department and was educated in computer science at MIT. She has 12 years of experience and specializes in tracking money throughout the world, from the Caymans to Zürich. She could backdoor any hidden account—a great person to have on a team for finding hidden funds.

The other person was Barney Yokem. Barney was an ex-marine, a pilot with several tours in combat. He can fly jets, twin-engine props, and helicopters. With over 10 years on the border, he's pretty much seen it all. Being an ex-lawman himself, Ben liked the idea of teaming up with him.

Ben contacted both Ms. Becker and Mr. Yokem and set up a meeting time and place for them to get to know each other and for him to get a status briefing. They all agreed on a restaurant on East Taylor Street, just to make sure that no one would be watching them. They are all aware that the people they will be tracking are dangerous folks. And, they will stop at nothing to survive.

They met at 11:00 a.m., to blend in with the lunch crowd. Ben arrived by cab about 20 minutes early, got an outside table with an umbrella, and ordered coffee. He had told the others that he would be wearing a red baseball cap.

As soon as he sat down, a lady approached. "Excuse me, do you happen to know a man named Ben?"

"My name is Ben. What can I do for you?"

"Hi, my name is Florence."

A typical intelligent-looking gal, her short hair complimented her jeans and light-blue, short-sleeved sweater. She didn't seem to have on any make-up and looked very much like a lady.

"Who sent you?" she asked.

"Martin. He thought I would be a good fit for the team."

"Wonderful," she said, waving at Barney Yokem who'd just arrived.

Barney was a tall, lanky guy, maybe 6'4", with a mustache. He could have used another 20 pounds. But he didn't look weak. He was wearing jeans, a long-sleeved white shirt, and cowboy boots. He talked with a southern drawl, from Alabama or Arkansas, Ben guessed. But he found out later that Barney was from Texas.

They sat outside and ate a chicken sandwich with lemonade, and shared pertinent details about their individual backgrounds and education. It didn't take long for them to feel secure and comfortable with each other.

"I know this must be strange for you, eating off the beating path" Florence said, "but it really is necessary. We wouldn't be the first to get hit by a sniper."

"I spent eight years with Texas DPS and some of that time was around the border, so I do appreciate what you are saying," Ben said, then added, "During my brief meeting with Martin, he indicated that you folks would provide me the details of the operation."

Florence began, "Well, we really don't have much yet, but the folks on the street are telling us that more and more product is being sold and the supply seems endless."

"What exactly is the product?"

"Primarily heroin, but cocaine has been moving too. They are moving heroin by the truckloads."

"How is it being moved into the U.S.? And how are they getting paid?"

"I'll leave the transporting discussion for Barney to fill in, but the money is being moved from the major distributors to a middleman who then deposits it in a few investment avenues for laundering. Their mark-up on the product is believed to be over 500%.

"We believe the primary West Coast laundering is being done through Multiple Family Investing, located in Seattle. The distributors collect from the dealers and then pass the cash to an organization that deposits the funds into an offshore account belonging to a shell company, which is used to invest the funds in Multiple Family Investing."

"So, they have it invested, but how do they get it out?"

Florence continued, "Multiple Family Investing is a subsidiary of a corporation home-based in Mexico City. A small amount of the funds is used to invest in apartments in Washington, Oregon, and California, but the remaining funds—we estimate 80%—is moved to the parent company in Mexico City. We also believe that the parent company in Mexico is owned by the major distributor that is supplying the heroin."

"Impressive. That's quite a financial trail. How much are we talking about?"

"We estimate that last year the total was in excess of one hundred billion dollars. So, if 80% went back to the distributor, that's quite a profit."

"For sure. Ok, I think I understand the financial side, how can I help?"

"Well, we were hoping that you might be able to investigate the operation of Multiple Family Investing and help us identify the incoming link to their cash flow, and any other companies involved within the U.S.

"We have not been able to get access to their books, but we have verified the movement of large sums of money moving through their bank accounts. Virtually all of their income is coming from the shell company, Island Distribution. We have not identified the owner of Island Distribution, but the account is held in the Cayman Islands."

"Well, I have done some work on Grand Cayman; I had a consulting contract with the police department a few years back. They wanted to get an idea for the cost of a public area camera system and some security for the government buildings. I spent about 10 days there; provided them a final report and three reputable security companies in the Houston area that were capable of providing the services, should they decide to complete the project. During that trip and a few dinner meetings in Houston, I made a couple of worthwhile contacts."

"Sounds good," she said, "Let's get together at the office tomorrow to formulate a starting point and some strategies."

"Great, how's 9:00 a.m.?" Ben suggested.

"Works for me; how about you, Barney?"

"Yeah, that's good."

Ben then turned to Barney. "Now, exactly how are they able to get the product into the U.S. without you guys catching them?"

"Oh," he said with a smile, "You're from Texas and ask me that? As you probably know, it's pretty easy.

"They have some slow twin engines that can land almost anywhere on very short runways, and they have helicopters to get to remote areas for transfer to the distributors with large trucks. You just can't be everywhere all the time."

Ben said, "I sure understand that. It's really frustrating when you are spending all night on a possible crossing just to find that they moved it by a different mode. They are true professionals."

Barney continued, "Currently, they are using private property to land and transfer to the helicopters, which will then hookup with the truckers in a hundred different locations in Prescott Valley, AZ, and north. They've been sighted as far north as Flagstaff. We've been able to bust a few of the trucks and obtain bits and pieces about the operation, but not much; and our hands are tied until we can get some local Public Safety folks involved."

"When will that be?" Ben asked.

"Our goal is to have at least 5 members from the Arizona Highway Patrol Investigative Department vetted within two weeks. We are looking for their finest officers with 3-to-5 years of experience."

"I would think that you would want a more seasoned member."

"Yeah," Barney said, "normally you would, but money becomes a major issue and history tells us that the cartels go after officers with more than five years of experience. Those officers have more control and more access to classified information about ongoing investigations. And they generally have larger families and the need for more money."

"It's sad, but true. On our border in Texas we rotated senior people every six months, just for security. What those officers don't initially realize is that when they start taking payoffs from the cartels, they are putting their whole family at risk."

"I know," Barney said, "but if you have financial problems and you are offered as much as ten times your annual salary just for a little information . . . well, you know how it goes. And we can get into more details during our meeting tomorrow morning."

They sat for a while and shared some additional, personal information about backgrounds and moving around with their families. About 1:00 p.m., they left for downtown. Ben rode with Barney back to the hotel. He wanted to get on his computer and try to contact some of the people he had worked with on the Cayman Islands project.

CHAPTER SEVEN

Patricia woke up with a resolved determination about her marriage. She had decided that she could not regain respect for Henry and that she would investigate the possibility of a divorce. Henry would be back from Chicago in a few days.

She was sure that he would not go quietly, because of his love for Michelle. That part, the child custody, would need to be worked out before things got too out of control.

Henry had already confessed to the affair with Bridget, his personal assistant. That fact had been shared with his brother, Arthur. And Arthur had shared it with JoAnn, so, the infidelity issue was not in question.

Patricia needed someone to discuss the situation with, so she called her best friend, JoAnn.

"Hello," JoAnn answered.

"Hi there. Do you have some time for a glass of wine at my place today or this evening?"

"Of course, I'm not available right now, but I could come by after 3:00 p.m. today; will that work?"

"That would be great! I'll pick up Michelle and head home. I'll see you then."

Patricia called Sara Whitney, a Family Law attorney. They had known each other for several years. Sara had worked a short while for Patricia's father's law firm in New York, but she and her husband decided to move to Atlanta for warmer winters.

"Hey, Patricia!" Sara said. "How are you?"

"I've been better, I'm afraid!"

"What's going on?"

"I have a personal issue that I would like to discuss with you. Are you available anytime soon?"

"Sure, I'm free right now, if you wish."

"That's good. I can be there by 1:30 p.m."

"That'll be great. See you then."

It was 12:15 p.m., and Sara's office was only about 20 minutes from Patricia's house. So she took a shower and dressed in jeans, a pullover shirt, and tennis shoes. She pulled her hair back in a ponytail and put on some minor makeup. She wasn't expecting to visit with anyone except Sara.

Patricia arrived at 1:20 p.m., and the secretary showed her into Sara's office. They had a light hug and a kiss on the cheek, and with big smiles said their "hellos."

Sara said, "Well, I'm sorry to find that you are having a problem. I hope I can help you. What's going on?"

"Well, my marriage has taken a turn for the worse," Patricia said. "Over the past year Henry has been having an affair with his personal assistant.

He admitted it a couple of months ago and we have been dealing with it ever since.

"He is out of town on business right now, so, I have decided to investigate the possibility of getting a divorce." She paused, "I just can't get it out of my head and I don't feel that I can trust him again."

"Oh my! I'm so sorry! But you don't sound like you are ready to file a formal divorce suit. Are there issues that you need clarification on before we start the formal process?"

"Could you just step me through the process? I've never handled a divorce case and never been even indirectly involved in one."

"Sure. First, we would want to identify the reason, then the financial settlement, including the home and personal items. Then, of course the child custody issue. That is generally the one that gets the most attention. Is Henry aware that you are considering a divorce?"

"No, he is too self-centered to think that I might take the initiative on such an important decision."

"Ok, we first have to formulate a 'to-do' list for you—things that you need to pull together to secure the case.

"You have to start off with the assumption that he will not cooperate and will fight you for everything. Now that isn't normally the case; but if you proceed with that mindset, then you are ready for any actions that he might decide to take.

"With his admission of guilt, you can expect the court to favor you, if there is a child custody battle. Therefore, we should focus on the financial issues. You have to make sure you are very thorough in identifying all assets, along with personal items that are important to you.

"I've seen people fight for months over the most insignificant things that were left out of the divorce decree, costing them both thousands of dollars in unnecessary legal fees, just because one party was not happy about getting a divorce or how it was settled. So, take your time and be thorough in identifying any and all items that you wish to keep."

Sara recognized the blank look of near defeat on Patricia's face. "Have you discussed this with anyone?"

"Not yet, but, I plan to talk it over with my best friend, JoAnn. She's coming to my house at 3:00 p.m. today for wine. She is married to Henry's brother, but we have been friends since college. We are very close."

"Ok. Try not to share the details with her or anyone else, other than your father!" She smiled at Patricia and said, "He is always your best go-to person. He loves you and is the best lawyer that I've ever known."

"Thank you! But I'm not ready for that conversation yet. I will most likely go up there for a visit after we get this process underway. I do want to talk with him and Mother about it; but not for advice regarding the details, just to let them know what's going on."

She laughed lightly then said, "I'm sure he will want me to come back to the firm and work with him. But I'm not ready for that either."

"Well, as I have told you before, there is a place for you in this law firm, if you ever want to work again."

"Thank you, but all of that is down the road. But I'll keep it in mind. Should we set up a follow-up appointment after I do my homework on the to-do list?"

"Yes, just call my office and let them know when you are ready for a meeting."

"Thanks, Sara, I'll see you soon."

"Take care, Patricia."

Patricia left the office and drove to the daycare, picked up Michelle, and went home.

It was a quarter till three and Patricia was looking forward to a visit with JoAnn. Mainly, she wanted to gain any information that JoAnn might have from Arthur about the affair.

CHAPTER EIGHT

After having a quick bite at the bar, Ben settled into his room with his computer wanting to contact a couple of people he had worked with on the Grand Cayman project.

First on his list was Frank Keith, a financial specialist with the Houston branch of Texas National Bank. Frank assisted Ben in the vetting of a contact on the island; an individual who had access to bank account identification throughout the island.

"Frank! How are you? Can't remember the last time we spoke. I hope everything is going well for you and your family."

"Yeah, everything is under control. We had another one, a little girl, about nine months ago; and Frank Jr. is now four. So, we have a full plate! But, it's all wonderful.

"What about you, Ben? What are you up to nowadays? Have you found anyone to settle down with?"

"Not really. I guess it's still just too early. But the reason I'm calling, Frank, is that I have a new client and it's kinda directing me toward the

Caymans. I thought maybe you would be able to help me; or direct me to someone who might help."

"I'll do what I can. What's up?"

"Well, I need some information about some shady dealings. My client is in the authority class, so I can't give you their name, but it's a heavy hitter. We have identified a shell corporation on the island and need to identify the owner and as many of their accounts as possible."

"I can try, Ben, what's the name of the shell?"

"Island Distribution."

"How fast do you need the info?"

"Well, we're having a strategy meeting next week, so if I could get something before then, it would be great."

"Ok, Ben, let me check around and I'll get back to you in a couple of days or so."

"Great, Frank, I appreciate the help and I'll wait for your call."

Ben opened his briefcase and took out all the papers pertaining to the case and placed them on the desk. Just as he sat down, there was a knock on the door. He unlocked the door and started opening it when someone from the other side pushed it hard—knocking him to the floor!

Two men in black clothes, masks, and hoodies rushed in. One stood over Ben, gun in hand, as the other one went straight for the briefcase; grabbing it and running to the door. The man over Ben struck him savagely in the head and followed the other man out of the room.

It took a few minutes for Ben to recover from the attack, but he quickly called 911 and reported the incident to the police and requested a detective be dispatched to take his statement.

Ben then called Barney to report the attack; obviously there had been a breach in security, someone knew that he was working with the AG's office. AND, they knew where he was staying, down to the room!

Barney arrived before the police and he and Ben went over the possibilities of who the attackers might have been and what they were after.

As luck would have it, Ben had saved all the relative information that he was carrying. However, the bad guys did get his identification information and a 9mm revolver.

Police Officer Smith and Detective McRae arrived in about 30 minutes. Ben gave a detailed statement and a list of what had been taken. He could only estimate their height and weight.

Detective McRae suggested Ben go to the hospital and get checked out, but Ben wasn't interested. He just wanted to focus on the issue at hand.

Then Officer Smith and Detective McRae left and told Ben that they would be in touch.

"Have you discussed the case with anyone?" Barney asked.

"No. I've only made one phone call since I've been here and I didn't identify the case or anyone that I was working with. These guys came into my room for one thing—my briefcase, nothing else."

"So if they were only interested in your briefcase; then they are involved with our case. So, who are they?"

They thought for a minute, then Barney said, "Well, I'm afraid we have a leak in our office. We need to backtrack and identify everyone that has knowledge of you coming to work on the case. It shouldn't take long, there's not that many involved."

"Well, I think it would be wise for me to move to another room. Would it be possible for me to get another weapon?"

"Sure, I'll check one out for you to carry while you're here. Just return it before you leave town."

"Ok, Barney, thanks."

Barney left for his office and Ben went to the front desk and spoke with the duty supervisor. "Would it be possible for me to change rooms? There was a security problem in my room and I would prefer changing rooms for now."

"Yes sir, let me check." The supervisor came back shortly and reassigned Ben to room 530.

Ben remembered that the lady that he had escorted to her room was in room 520. Also, she was the only person that would have known what room he was in.

Ben called the front desk and asked to speak with Ms. Harding in room 520. The clerk said, "I'm sorry, Mr. Berkshire, but Ms. Harding checked out this morning."

Ben immediately called Barney; "I believe I know how the two guys knew my hotel and room number." Ben briefly went over the meeting and dinner he had with Lois Harding.

"Ok, I'll get someone in Boston to investigate Ms. Harding and her family; if that is her real name."

"Sounds good. I'm gonna get some shuteye. But, man! I have to say, if she is a fake, she is really good!"

It was after 10:00 p.m., and Ben decided to shower and call it a night.

CHAPTER NINE

Around 8:45 a.m., Ben arrived at Florence Becker's office. He was immediately shown in and Barney was already there. "Good morning, Florence, Barney."

"Good morning, Ben, how's the head? I understand that you had some visitors last night!"

"Yeah, a couple of unfriendly fellows made a brief stop! But it worked out ok."

"Good morning, Ben," Barney said, "Did you get any rest?"

"Yeah, I changed rooms to 530, and secured the door, so I slept well."

"We should be hearing something from Boston sometime today, good or bad," Barney said, and took a sip from his steaming coffee. "It would be a surprise if she used her real name. From what you told us, she could be a real pro."

"I agree. She really sucked me in, for sure."

"Ok," said Florence, "back to the case. Ben, were you able to make any progress on contacting someone in the Caymans?"

"No, not yet, but I have a friend in Houston working on it. He's a banker that I've worked with before and he's attempting to make a contact on the island for us. Should hear something tomorrow or so."

"Ok, how can we proceed?" Florence asked.

"Well, I'm not sure that we can, until I get a call from my contact. However, I think that it would be worthwhile to look into the possible leak here or at Barney's office. This Ms. Harding is working for someone, and that someone got very accurate information about the case and about me through one of the two offices, don't you agree?"

"Yes. Barney and I were discussing the situation before you arrived. We are backtracking the flow of information to identify all the people that might have knowledge relative to this specific case."

"I'll get back to you as soon as I get a response from my contact in Houston. Let me know if I can be of any help."

"Ok, Ben, you heading back to the hotel?"

"Yes."

"Let me walk you out. I have something for you in my car." Barney gave him a 9mm Beretta and had him sign for it. They talked for a few minutes and Ben went back to the hotel.

Ben tracked down the Security Manager of the hotel, a Mr. Donald Wilbur. He gave Mr. Wilbur a detailed report on the incident in his room.

"Would it be possible for us to check out room 520? Ms. Harding may have left clues as to her identity or where she might be heading next."

"You bet!" Mr. Wilbur got on his radio and verified the status of the room; it was empty. They entered the room and housekeeping had not arrived so it was just as Ms. Harding had left it.

A search of the bed, table, and desk revealed nothing. Then Ben noticed the corner of a business card sticking out from under the desk leg. He pulled it out and carefully handed it to Mr. Wilbur. They put it in a plastic container then took a closer look.

The name was Juanita Cruz, Attorney General's office. Ms. Harding's contact was higher up than we thought! We searched the bathroom and found hair and a broken fingernail. We bagged the items and left.

"I'll turn this evidence over to Detective McRae," Mr. Wilbur said.

"Thank you."

Ben called Florence and Barney and shared the latest with them. Florence was to follow up on Ms. Cruz.

Ben decided to take a few hours off and try to clear his head and regroup. This situation was getting rough faster than he had anticipated. He just could not figure out why his involvement would be so important to anyone this early in the game. The rest of the day was spent working out the details for tracking the money.

CHAPTER TEN

Florence called Assistant AG Martin Perez. "Good morning, Martin. I hope all is well this fine morning."

"Well, good morning, Florence. Yes, we think that we have everything under control. Yet, here you are on the phone," he said with a little laugh.

She laughed too. "Nothing you can't handle, Martin; just a little detective work."

"We're opening a very big money case. We've brought in a high profile investigator to help us. His first night here, he was attacked in his hotel room and all that the robbers wanted was his briefcase.

"So I thought of you because there is an indication that someone in your area might have been involved with feeding the robbers information on the investigator and where he was staying."

"Who is the investigator?"

"Ben Berkshire."

"Oh, yeah, I know him. And he was here meeting with the boss yesterday or the day before."

"Great. We need your help to look at a Ms. Juanita Cruz as a possible mole."

"Why Juanita?"

"Her business card was found in the room of a person of interest that had contact with Ben prior to him going to his room."

"Got it. I'll check out her background, personnel file, and work history with us. Shouldn't take long. What was the person of interest's name?"

"A Ms. Lois Harding from Boston—if that's her real name."

He told Florence that he would contact her before the day was out.

Martin hung up and contacted the HR Director, Ms. Wanda Givings. He brought her up to speed on the situation and directed her to do a thorough behind-the-scene investigation of Ms. Cruz, ASAP!

Turned out that Ms. Cruz was hired about a year earlier and her prior address was Chicago where she worked for Title One Real Estate Investment Company—one of the companies Florence had identified to Ben during their initial meeting.

But that didn't connect her to Ms. Harding, who said that she was from Boston.

Ms. Givings contacted the AG office in Boston and asked them to trace a Ms. Lois Harding.

Within the hour, she got a call from Boston and they verified that a Ms. Lois Harding lived in Boston, was in the fashion design business, and was from a prominent Boston family.

She called Mr. Perez and shared the findings with him.

Well, that does thicken the plot! How does Ms. Cruz know Ms. Harding? Mr. Perez thought.

"Ok, you keep all this under close wrap; and since Ms. Cruz works here with me, I will figure out a way to investigate her without her knowing about our discovery.

"Also, please get back to the Boston AG office and get more information about Ms. Harding and her family—things like her father's name, any family businesses, family travels out this way and also to Seattle and the Cayman Islands."

"Yes sir, I'll find out what I can."

"Great, thanks."

Martin called Florence and passed on what he had found out. He suggested that maybe the best approach to Ms. Cruz would be by the police. Since the business card had been found in Ms. Harding's room; it would be natural for a detective to contact Ms. Cruz.

Florence contacted Detective McRae and shared the information with him and requested that he contact Ms. Cruz to see if he could determine exactly what the relationship, if any, was between the two women.

Detective McRae called Ms. Cruz at her office and requested that she come by his office to discuss a case that he was currently investigating.

"How could I possibly be of any assistance?" Ms. Cruz asked.

"Well, your name has come up in my investigation and I would like to have an interview with you, if you don't mind. I would hate to come to your office for the interview, since you work for the Assistant AG."

"Sure, I'll drop by in the morning."

"That will be fine, say around 10:00 a.m., and thanks for your cooperation."

Detective McRae then called Ben.

"Hi, Detective, what's up?"

"Well, we may have a break in your case. It has to do with Ms. Cruz at the Assistant AG's office. I will be interviewing Ms. Cruz tomorrow morning around 10:00 a.m. and thought you might want to be here. I can't include you in the interview, but you could listen in on the other side of a two-way."

"Yeah, that would be great. I'll be there for sure."

"Ok, Ben, see you tomorrow."

The interview started off pretty routine—prior places she had lived, what type of education she had, what city she came from, and how she came to be employed by the AG's office. Nothing remarkable showed up.

Then the detective asked her, "Do you know a Ms. Lois Harding?"

Ms. Cruz squirmed in her seat and rubbed her hands together before she answered. "Well, I think that I might have met her around town."

Detective McRae paid no attention to her physical reactions and pushed on. "Please try to remember, if you can, exactly where you might have met her."

"I think that I might have met her at the Hyatt hotel, downtown."

"And when would that have been?"

"A few days ago, I was at the bar, we were talking and she said that she was having a get-together in her room; she invited me up as part of a group."

"While you two were at the bar, what did you talk about?"

"Just light-hearted things—fun, parties, men."

"Any specific men?"

"No, not really."

"Did a Mr. Ben Berkshire's name come up?"

"Ms. Cruz got uncomfortable again, "I'm not sure."

"Oh, come on, Ms. Cruz," he said, with a little more force, "you must remember the men that you two talked about."

"Well, there was one guy that she talked about; his name might have been Ben. She had had dinner with him and was impressed. She thought that he was cute and sexy. But he didn't show any interest in her, so she came to the bar to meet her friends."

"Had you ever heard the name Ben Berkshire before?"

"No, I have never met him."

"I didn't ask you if you had met him, I asked if you had heard of him. Prior to your meeting with Ms. Harding, had you ever heard his name?"

"No, I don't think so, why?"

"We're just trying to tie up some loose ends. You said that you were from Chicago, where did you work before coming to Arizona?"

"I was an agent at a real estate company."

"A sales agent?"

"No, I was in their research department."

"What was the name of the company?"

"Title One."

"And what exactly does Title One do?"

"They find desirable places to build apartment projects. I was one of the people that sifted through government records and found locations where land could be purchased at a discounted rate."

"And how long did you work at Title One?"

"About three years."

"Where did you work before that?"

"I was in Mexico City going to school and working at a club."

"How did you wind up in the U.S.?"

"My boss at the club where I worked helped me through school and then recommended me for the job with Title One."

"Who owns Title One?"

"I'm not sure but I believe the owners are in Mexico."

"When did you come to Phoenix?"

"About a year and a half ago."

"Why?"

"To get a job in the government."

"Ms. Cruz, I am now going to swear you in, and after that, anything that you say can and will be used against you in a court of law. Do you understand?"

"Yes, but I don't know why! I haven't done anything wrong! Maybe I need a lawyer?"

Detective McRae swore her in and told her that she had a right to have a lawyer; but if she has nothing to hide, she really didn't need one.

"Now, Ms. Cruz..." He paused.

Detective McRae noticed that the indicator light came one, which meant that someone on the other side of the glass wanted to speak with him.

He excused himself and stepped outside. "What is it, Ben?"

"Ask her if she still has contact with the people at Title One. If so, if they gave her any instructions regarding me."

"Ok, I will."

Detective McRae returned to the interrogation room.

"Ms. Cruz please remember that you are under oath and a failure to tell the truth could result in you going to prison; and that everything that is said in this room is recorded. Do you understand that?"

"Yes!"

"Ok, now, do you still have contact with the people at Title One?"

"Yes."

"What is your involvement with them?"

"I do some research for them sometimes. They ask me to checkout different people and provide information about them."

"What people?"

"People associated with the AG's office."

"Were you asked to check into Mr. Ben Berkshire?"

"No, but as a routine report, I report to them on anyone who comes to the AG's office from out of town. I reported to them on the arrival of Mr. Berkshire from Atlanta."

"In what context?"

"Who he met with and where he was staying."

"Do you still have contact with the owner of the club in Mexico City where you worked?"

"No, he is very important."

"Now, back to your visit with Ms. Harding, did you talk with her about Mr. Berkshire?"

"Yes, she told me that he was in the private investigating business, and what room he was staying in."

"Ms. Cruz, I am now going to place you under arrest for conspiring to breaking and entering resulting in the attack on Mr. Berkshire. I believe that you should contact your lawyer."

Ms. Cruz's eyes begin to fill with tears and her body was shaking.

Detective asked an officer to take Ms. Cruz to Booking.

CHAPTER ELEVEN

The next morning, while having coffee at the hotel, Ben thought that maybe he could get some answers from Ms. Harding. He pulled out her card and dialed her number in Boston but it rolled over to another number.

"Good morning, this is Lois Harding, how may I help you?"

"Hi Lois! It's Ben Berkshire, we met in Phoenix a few days ago."

"Oh yes! Wow! Great to hear from you, Ben! I was going to contact you soon."

"I had to leave Phoenix suddenly because of some family issues here in Boston. Are you still in Phoenix?"

"Yes, I am. And a lot happened on the night you left and since then."

He gave her a general outline of what happened without any great details.

"My, my! Are you ok?"

"Yes, I'm fine. But I wanted to ask you if you remember meeting a young lady at the hotel by the name of Cruz, Juanita Cruz."

"Yes! After you abandoned me at my door," she laughed, "I decided to reconnect with my friends at the bar and we then went back to my room for a while. I met Juanita at the bar while I was waiting for my friends. She was very sweet and friendly. I even invited her up to our brief little party. That's when I got the call from home and had to pack and head to the airport."

"Did Ms. Cruz give you a business card?"

"Yes, she did; but I believe that I left it on a table when I cleared the room. What does she have to do with what happened to you?"

"I'm not sure if she has anything to do with what happened. I'm just trying to connect the dots."

"Well, I'm afraid I can't help you there; I only spent a couple of hours with her."

"Well, thanks for the info. Is everything with the family under control?"

"Oh yes! Just some confusion," she said, laughing. "There's always lots of drama in this family. Will your travels ever bring you up this way? Boston is a beautiful place to visit."

"I know, I've been through there a few times. Maybe I'll be seeing you one day. But I thought that your business was in New York?"

"It is, but I'm at home for a while and thinking about moving everything up here."

"Interesting. Ok then, thanks for clearing things up. I better get back to work. We should keep in touch."

"That would be great," she said.

Ben immediately called Detective McRae and passed on the information he got from his conversation with Ms. Harding.

"Well, that pretty much rules her out of the equation."

"Yeah, I thought so too, but I'll keep in contact with her, just in case."

"Good idea. Well, the big million-dollar question is, how did they tie you to the secret investigation with Florence and Barney?"

"I suppose that she reported my arrival to Title One."

"Yeah, and they had the two goons break into your room to get the briefcase."

"That sounds about right," Ben agreed.

They hung up and Ben ordered a light breakfast.

Ben was finishing up his breakfast. It was about 10:30 a.m., and he wanted to get a shower and try to meet up with Barney to go over some security ideas.

He noticed the doorknob moving, so he slipped over to the side table and retrieved his 9mm and dropped beside the bed.

The door opened slowly and two men, all in black walked in, guns in hand. Ben aimed at them and told them to drop their weapons. One of the men pointed his weapon at Ben.

Ben fired, hitting the guy in the chest, driving him back, his head hitting the floor hard.

The other man fired twice at Ben but didn't have enough of a target to hit him.

Ben then fired twice and hit him in the chest.

Both men were down in the hallway.

Ben checked them to make sure they were out of the fight and picked up their weapons.

Several guests were peeking out of their doors. Ben told one of them, "Call 911 and the front desk for the security officer of the hotel."

Within minutes, Security Officer Wilbur showed up. He saw Ben and the two men. He first checked the two men for life.

Then he turned to Ben, "Are you ok?"

"Yeah, they could be the same two guys that broke into my room. But I couldn't identify them."

After close inspection, it was determined that the two men were Hispanic. A check of their wallets revealed that both were from Mexico City.

The city police arrived and within a few minutes Detective McRae was on scene. McRae said to Ben, with a smile, "Damn, man! Do you always have a dark cloud following you?"

"Only since I arrived in your fair city," Ben said, with a smile. "We checked out those two, and they are from Mexico City. So, I would assume that they are part of that group that the AAG is interested in."

The CSI team showed up and did their thing; then released the bodies to the coroner, who had them bagged, tagged, and moved out of the hotel to the morgue.

Mr. Wilbur started inspecting the room for bullet holes for his report.

Ben and McRae moved out onto the balcony and closed the door behind them.

McRae said, "I'm sure that I don't have to tell you that this is just the beginning. Someone wants you off this case, and in a serious way."

"Yeah, I'm getting that feeling!"

"By now, they know a lot about you and your life and most likely your family."

Ben looked out at the parking lot and saw Barney moving slowly from this car.

"Did you call Barney, Detective?"

"Yes, we know each other."

"Ok, thanks."

Barney walked out on the balcony to join them. He smiled and said, "Hey Ben, how's it going?"

"Just fine."

"Looks like the weapon works ok."

"Yep!" Ben said with a smile.

McRae said, with a laugh, "You get two Texans together and you don't get much said.

Barney smiled then looked at Ben. "My instinct says that it might be wise for you to go back to Atlanta and regroup while Florence and I assess the situation here and develop a tactical strategy plan."

"Well, as long as I'm here, I don't mind the inconvenience. But it's up to you guys."

"Well," Barney said, "You're not gonna be much good to anyone now; your cover is blown and they will focus on you till you are neutralized."

"You could be right, but I think we need to discuss it with Florence."

Barney agreed.

Ben put a call in to Florence. She was unavailable, so he left a message with her office.

"How about that chicken place for some lunch?" Barney suggested.

"Great, I'll be there in about an hour.

Ben rolled up to the chicken place and drove around it a couple of times, checking out all the cars and their tags and occupants. Nothing stood out. He got out of the car and settled into an outside corner table. Barney drove up, looked around, and took a seat next to Ben; both having their backs against the wall.

Ben spent about 15 minutes sharing all that he could remember about what had happened at the hotel. When he was finished, Barney smiled and said, "You having fun yet?" A typical response from a guy that had been under fire and in many combat situations.

Ben laughed, "More than I anticipated! It's apparent that I have a target on my back now; so, I'm wondering just how effective I can be out here."

"Yeah, that's a good question for sure. And I don't want the problem to spread to your family."

"I'm going to let Florence discuss it with the AAG, but I'm sure her response will be in agreement with our assessment." He paused for few minutes then said, "I plan to return to Atlanta for a short while, then go to Houston. I will continue to work my contacts there to obtain information on the activity in the Caymans. You and Florance can let me know what our next step will be."

"Sounds good, Ben. Be safe. I'll pass it on to Florence, and if you need any backup or support, you have my private number. I have support contacts all over."

"Got it! Thanks." He went back to his hotel to pack for his return to Atlanta.

CHAPTER TWELVE

After Patricia left her attorney's office and picked up Michelle, she drove home to meet with JoAnn at 3:00 p.m. She wanted to discuss in more detail Henry's involvement with his assistant, and to what degree JoAnn was aware of the affair, and for how long.

JoAnn, in a general way, had previously acknowledged knowing about the affair but never shared any details.

Patricia was sure that it was because she didn't want to interfere with her marriage. But now that it was out in the open, Patricia was hoping that JoAnn would share all that she knew. The more that she could gather, the more she could share with her attorney.

At 2:50 p.m., JoAnn came into the house and said, "Hey there, how are you doing?"

Patricia hugged her and said, "Oh, I'm doing ok; just been pretty busy trying to figure everything out and what my next move will be."

Patricia poured them a glass of wine. "Here's to the future," JoAnn said, raising her glass.

Patricia smiled and said, "Yeah! Whatever that might be." They tipped glasses and drank, then settled on the couch.

"Well, I had my first meeting with Sara, my attorney today."

"I remember her. I think that I met her here at your place once."

"Yeah, she has been here several times at parties. I've known her for a long time. She once worked for my dad's firm in New York. She has a small firm here in Atlanta, doing quite well."

"Anyway, she mapped out what she needed from me to proceed with a divorce, and gave me a To-Do list for accumulating the necessary information."

"So, you're pretty sure this is what you want to do?"

"I think so! It has really been difficult to live with Henry this last year or so; knowing that he was sleeping with someone else." Tears begin to well up in her eyes. "And I was being neglected and rejected. I've had such a rough time, JoAnn, and I have been so lonely, not having anyone to talk with about my heartbreak."

"Oh, my dear! I'm so sorry! I should have talked about it with you a long time ago. But I just didn't know how to, or what to say—I just knew it would break your heart."

"I understand; but now, I need for you to tell me everything that you know. I don't want to get blindsided during these next few months while we are in the process of getting this divorce."

"I'm ready to help you. What do you need from me?"

"First, I need to know exactly when it started and just how much time he has been spending with her. Also, if possible, any information that would indicate his intention to leave me for her. And, will the information that you share with me be that which has come from Arthur?"

"Yes, all that I know has come from Arthur. I don't believe that Henry is aware that I have any knowledge of his affair, but he has been very open with Arthur. And, since they work together, Arthur has firsthand knowledge of their involvement."

"When did the affair start?"

"According to Arthur, the flirting and touching started almost a year and a half ago. But their physical affair only started about 13 months ago. They started leaving the office for several hours together. And in time, they started having dinners and openly dating." JoAnn took a sip from her glass and continued, "During the past few months, Arthur has indicated that Henry was considering leaving you, but just wasn't ready to give up Michelle."

"Wow! How stupid and naïve I've been!"

"Henry led Arthur to believe that he had sex with her a few times, but he was trying to break it off."

"Damn! And all the time he was getting more involved with her!"

"I'm so sorry, my dear!"

"Thank you. Are you aware of any of the places that they stayed?"

"Let's see, I believe that Arthur once mentioned The Westin at Peachtree Plaza, and the Marriott on Peachtree, and the Marquis."

"Thanks for this information. And could you get her cell number for me? I don't intend to call her, but I'm sure that my attorney will want to check out some phone records."

"Sure. I think Arthur should have it in his briefcase."

"All of this is very helpful, JoAnn. I truly appreciate your support. I'm so relieved to have a friend with whom I can share this problem. And, with someone I can trust."

"Again, I'm truly sorry that I didn't tell you sooner. But I was hoping that everything would work out."

Patricia checked on Michelle, she was fast asleep. They had more wine and talked about this and that for an hour or so.

Finally, JoAnn said, "I have to get home. I'll give you a call tomorrow, and I'll keep you aware of anything that I hear."

"Thanks again."

They hugged and promised to get back together soon.

CHAPTER THIRTEEN

After everyone left, Ben secured his room and called his office in Atlanta. His assistant got all the necessary information from him to book his flight and have someone pick him up at the airport.

At 1:00 p.m. he dialed Patricia's number.

"Hello?"

"Hi there! How's everything on the home front?"

"Oh! Hi, Ben! It's so good to hear your voice! Are you back home?"

"No, I'm still in Phoenix, but I'm heading home later today. Are you free for lunch tomorrow?"

"Absolutely!"

"Ok then, I'll give you a call in the morning and we'll pick a place."

"Sounds wonderful! See you tomorrow!"

Ben called the AAG, Martin Perez, and had a brief conversation with him about the general situation and that he would be going back to Atlanta for a while to begin working on a different leg of the investigation.

Mr. Perez agreed that it was the best decision and told Ben that he would inform him of any changes in Phoenix.

Ben's flight out of Phoenix was at 4:10 p.m. and with the three-and-a-half-hour-flight time, plus the loss of three more hours in time zones, he expected to arrive in Atlanta a little before 11:00 p.m.

The flight was uneventful and Ben was able to get some sleep. When he arrived in Atlanta his car was waiting. The driver was a guy that he knew and they had a light chat on the way to Ben's place.

Ben had left Tula with an excellent doggie hotel where the dogs are separated by size and are able to sleep on large pillows, chairs, and couches. A great place; and Tula liked the lady that managed it.

Since it was late, he decided to pick her up the next day.

He checked his mail, which was stacked on a table just inside the front door. The housekeeper had picked it up at his P.O. box.

Nothing urgent jumped out at him, so he went to his bedroom to unpack and get a shower before enjoying his own bed for a change.

Around 7:00 a.m., the alarm went off. Apparently, he had not shut it off before he left, and it had been set for 7:00 a.m. each day. But he was rested and ready for the day, so he got up.

He made some coffee and opened some of the mail; separating junk from bills and tossing the junk.

Having his own coffee in his own cup—well, that was nice, really nice!

At 10:00 a.m., Ben left to go pick up Tula. She was so happy to see him, she couldn't stand still! He held her, kissed her, and rubbed her little belly. She was so sweet!

He let her run around the office while he paid the bill, then they left for home. During the ride, Tula couldn't get close enough to Ben. She really missed him!

After they got home, Ben took Tula for a nice walk and then gave her a couple of treats. She settled in to her normal routine at home and quickly forgot about the hotel she'd just left. Ben finished with the mail, logged into his online bank account, and paid a few bills.

Later, he called Patricia and chatted for a few minutes. She recommended having lunch at the club. He asked her if Henry was back from Chicago, and she said, "No." That was good; made it simpler to have a visit without any hassle. They agreed to meet at for lunch at 1:00 p.m. the following day.

He had several days of newspapers to read, so he took a seat in the den, which was facing the front of the house with a window view of the street. He normally read his paper there, early in the morning with his coffee.

As he was reading the paper, he heard a car out front and looked out the window, through the curtains. It was a dark 4-door sedan and it stopped just past his house, lights still on, with the engine running. He wasn't able to count the number of people in the car. But the driver's window was down and he could tell that the man was looking toward his house.

Ben got up, grabbed a 9mm that he kept at the front door and opened the door, stepping just outside into the yard. The man in the car looked for a few seconds, rolled up his window and they slowly drove away. The tag was not a Georgia tag, but Ben wasn't able to clearly see where it was from.

He went back into the house and stayed out of view but in a position that allowed him to clearly see the street. After 30 minutes or so, he decided that the car wasn't coming back right away. He called Barney.

"Hey, Barney, how's everything going?

"Well, it was ok, until I got this call," he said, with a slight laugh. "What kind of trouble have you found now?"

"Oh, you are getting to know me too well. I'm at my house, and noticed a strange car out front. But when I went outside, they drove away. Didn't get a tag, but it wasn't from Georgia."

"Ok, I'll have some of our people keep an eye on the house, especially when you aren't home and at night." He gave Ben a number to call in case he needed immediate backup.

"You don't think the local guys would be better?"

"No, Ben, we don't know 'who is who' right now. But we do know that our people have been vetted and are on our side. Your contact will be a guy called Corbin, not his real name, but everyone knows him as Corbin. He is ex-special ops and I have trusted him with my life on more than one occasion. He also has an excellent team in the North Georgia district, with a home base in Atlanta. And I have already passed on the necessary information to him."

"The safe identification words between you and Corbin and his team is STONE MOUNTAIN. You can expect them to use it immediately when making contact with you. They will expect you to do the same."

"Holy shit, Barney! Do you really think that this level of security is necessary?"

"I do."

"Ok, then, I'll take your lead! But I have to have some control in this."

"That isn't a problem, I know that this isn't your first rodeo, Ben, but let me get the people in contact with you and they will be able to set up the plan and you can work with Corbin on the control aspect."

"Ok then, I'll wait to hear from Corbin."

"Ben! Don't underestimate these people. We have had contact with them before. They are really bad guys with heavy fire power."

"Yeah, ok. I've been on easy street for a long time. I'll just have to gear up for a little action."

"By the way, do you still have my 9mm?"

"No, I gave it to Detective McRae to return to you."

"Ok, thanks. Be safe, Ben!"

"Will do!"

CHAPTER FOURTEEN

Florence and Barney arrived at the AAG's office for a planning session. Since Ben left, Florence had been able to identify some small banks that the distributor was using to move funds. It seemed that more money than usual was moving to the Caymans.

It was generally believed that the larger banks were getting concerned about the volume of money flowing through their accounts. Such increases could cause the Feds to tag them as a risk and place them in an investigation posture, resulting in the takeover of the bank by the IRS or the local government's regulatory arm.

AAG Perez was concerned about a recent report from Barney which indicated that more product was moving into Arizona and on to Chicago. Their contact in Chicago reported that the funds in the Title One accounts had been significantly increased. And the local county records indicated that Title One is making large land purchases for the development of apartment projects, which provides them more opportunity to launder the incoming funds.

It was agreed that Ben should go to the Caymans and investigate the shell company, Island Distribution. Barney would take a team into the Prescott Valley and try to disrupt the flow of heroin, and Florence would work with Ben on the Cayman trip.

Florence called Ben.

"Ben Berkshire."

"Hi, Ben, Florence here. I just need to discuss your next step in this project."

"Ok. Right now, I plan to visit my friend in Houston and, through him, make contact with someone on the main island. Are there any new developments in your area?"

"Yes, but we can talk about that later. What can I do to help you regarding the Cayman trip?"

"Not much, everything is kind of depending on us being able to make a firm contact down there. I should know more about that in a couple of days."

"Ok, Ben, just keep me in the loop. Oh, also, there seems to be a lot of activity in Chicago. And I need you to purchase some burner phones so we can talk more freely, in case these phones are being tapped. I have a secure phone in my office, and I will purchase some burners also, and pass the numbers to you on my secure phone."

"Sounds good. I have a second phone now, too. The number is xxx-xxx-xxxx. You can text the number of your first burner phone to that phone, then I will toss it and call you with a new burner phone. Does that make sense?"

"Yes, Ben. Thanks."

"Ok. I'll pass the number to you when I get to my office."

"Be safe, Ben. Barney says that things are going to heat up very soon."

"Will do!"

In about an hour, Florence texted the number of her new burner phone to Ben from her secure office phone, and he went to the phone store and purchased five burner phones. He called Florence on her new burner phone.

"Ok. Now back to Barney. He is taking a team to the Prescott Valley for a major strike on the incoming product runners, mainly heroin, we believe. It could be a significant blow to their distribution into Chicago. So be careful, it might blow back on you, since you are the only other contact that they have identified thus far."

"Roger that!"

Ben hung up and called his contact, Frank Keith, in Houston.

"Frank here."

"Hi, Frank, it's Ben in Atlanta."

"Hi, Ben, you are on my list to call. I have a name for you on the island. She has been working with us for several years and has been vetted by the Feds. I think that you can trust her. She is a secret agent for the Justice Department."

"Great, what's her name? And, by the way, this is a burner that I'm on. So you might be getting calls from unidentified numbers over the next few weeks because I'll be changing phones as requested by my client."

"Ok, no problem." He gave Ben the information on the contact in the Caymans.

"Her name is Beatrice Farmer, and she is employed by Cayman National Bank as a senior financial advisor. She has been there for four years. Her time zone is only one hour behind yours. So she's on Houston time."

"Did you notify her that I might be calling?"

"No, not yet, but I will do that today. So starting tomorrow, you should be able to make contact with her. Are you going down there?"

"Yes, but I'm not sure exactly when; it might be a few days."

"Who and what would you like for me to introduce you as?"

"Well, I suppose I should be looking for a safe place to put my money, since she is a financial advisor."

"That would work, and it would justify her spending some time with you. We don't want to jeopardize her position."

The next morning, Ben called Ms. Farmer.

"Good morning, Beatrice Farmer."

"Good morning, Ms. Farmer, my name is Ben Berkshire and I got your name from Frank Keith."

"Yes, Mr. Berkshire, I have spoken with Mr. Keith. You come highly recommended."

"Well, thank you. And, please, call me Ben."

"Very well, Ben, and you may call me Beatrice."

"Thank you, Beatrice. I have some financial matters that I believe you might be able to advise me on. Would you be available sometimes in the next few days if I made a trip to the island?"

"Of course, Ben. I will look forwarding to meeting you. What day would be good for you?"

"Well, today is Friday, so maybe next Tuesday, if that works for you."

"That would be excellent. You have my number, so text me your flight and hotel information when you have completed your schedule. Then I can block out some time to spend with you while you are here."

"Excellent! See you then."

It was getting close to noon so Ben called Patricia.

"Good morning, Ben! How does your day look?"

"I'm pretty busy, but I was thinking of you and wondering if you wanted to have lunch."

"Yeah, that would be great. Michelle doesn't get out of school until 3:00 p.m."

"Ok, then, and secondly, when do you expect Henry home?"

"Tomorrow or the next day; he said something about his client giving him a ride back on their private plane."

"Nice! Who is his client in Chicago?"

"I'm not sure. He really doesn't share much of his business with me. I believe though that it's some real estate company. But I have no idea what the name is."

"Do you normally pick him up?"

"No, he just parks his car at the airport."

"Ok, what's your fancy for lunch?"

"Most anything light. I'm hoping that someone is taking me to dinner tonight."

He smiled. "Oh, you are, are you! Well, if he doesn't work out, maybe I could fill in."

"You're a perfect backup!" She chuckled, "I just love being around you, Ben Berkshire!"

He laughed and said, "Well, you are a delight for these old eyes. Let's have lunch at Willie's BBQ. They have a great western salad bar and I'll have a lean brisket sandwich with some beans and cold slaw."

"No backing off for you today!"

"I'm tough and need energy." He laughed. "Should I pick you up?"

"No, I'll just meet you there, say 1:30 p.m., and I can just pick up Michelle from there."

"Ok, I'll see you there. Keep smiling!"

"I will," she laughed a little and hung up.

Ben called Florence next.

"Hi, Ben."

"I have a very good contact on the island and I'll be visiting her next Tuesday. She works for the Justice Department."

"Excellent, maybe you can obtain some direct knowledge about the flow of cash going through Island Distribution."

"I hope so. I'll keep you up to speed. When is Barney making his move?"

"Tonight, I believe. I haven't received a go-ahead from the AAG, but it should be tonight. I'll give you a head's up."

"Ok, I'll be ready."

Ben hung up and headed over to Willie's BBQ to meet Patricia. He was looking forward to seeing her and having some light-hearted conversation and a few laughs.

He saw her shiny Mercedes in the parking lot, parked next to it, and walked inside.

Patricia was standing just inside and broke into a big smile and gave him a big hug and a kiss, on the lips.

Ben reciprocated and then took her hand, walked to the reception area, and gave them his name. They were immediately seated. The lunch crowd had thinned out, so there was plenty of room.

They sat across from each other, looking into each other's eyes, smiling and thinking their separate wonderful thoughts. "So what have you been doing all morning, Ben?"

"Oh, this and that, nothing of any great importance. Trying to get a trip to the Caymans set up for next Tuesday. I have a client issue that requires me to go down there for a couple of days. You want to go?" he said, with a big smile.

"I'd love to! But I'm pretty much tied down here for a while, with this divorce case about to break open and Michelle's school. But I'll take a rain check on a trip!"

"That's a deal. Anytime! When do you expect to serve Henry?"

"I suppose sometime next week. It all depends on how fast I can accumulate the information that Sara needs."

"How's that going?"

"Very well, actually."

"Our home records are well organized and I was able to gather the details on all our assets. So, I just have the personal stuff left, which I plan to do first thing tomorrow, before Henry returns. And then package it up for Sara. She says that all the phone records have been obtained and she has an investigator in her office formulating a detailed report for us."

"How do you think he will take it?"

'Well, I suppose that he will be dumbfounded, because he will be totally surprised that I have taken the initiative to file. But, it won't take long for the realization to set in. In the filing I'm requiring him to immediately move out. With the primary cause being adultery, Sara believes that the judge will pretty much give me whatever I request.

"First things will be him moving out, my access to our finances, and my vehicle. And total custody of Michelle. But he is a pretty hostile man, and if he gets upset, he will attempt to retaliate. So, Sara and I don't expect it to go without a challenge.

"But frankly, I don't give a damn! I'm tired of his mad outbursts and intimidating attacks. I'm not afraid of him and refuse to take anymore from him."

"That's a very healthy attitude, my dear, and I will be very close, if you need me."

"Thanks, Ben, I know that, and it really does give me strength."

"Good."

They ate and talked about where to have dinner and made a joke here and there. It was a happy time in both of their lives.

She could see some better times ahead and he was feeling that, *MAYBE* there was a chance they could build something together.

CHAPTER FIFTEEN

Around 5:00 p.m., Ben received a call from Florence saying that Barney and his group would be making their move about 11:00 p.m., their time (midnight, Ben's time). Barney had a small tactical group of 10 to 12 men. All were special forces trained. Their objective was to take down the distribution gang and take possession of the product.

They were expecting a heavy firefight.

If their Intel was correct, the product would be moved by helicopter from aircrafts in the Phoenix area to the Prescott Valley location. Then it would be moved on to Chicago by semitrailer trucks.

Ben called Corbin.

"Hi, Ben, what's up?"

"How did you know it was me? I'm on a burner!"

"Funny man! Florence keeps us informed on any changes that are implemented, including phones, security codes, and vehicles. According to my guys, you haven't been home all day, and everything seems to be normal."

"Good to know, thanks, Corbin. So, I'm sure you are aware of the activity in Arizona."

"Yep."

"Barney told me earlier that when it goes down, I should be especially vigilant."

"We've got your back. Do you expect to be home tonight?"

"Yes, but I'm having dinner out, then I should be home around 10:00 p.m."

"Ok, then. If you need help or have any concerns, just call me."

"Ok, Corbin, thanks again."

"You bet! And tell your lady friend hi from us!"

"What lady?"

Corbin laughed, "Really? You think we are just a bunch of mercenaries? We're keeping an eye on you!"

Ben chuckled, "Fair enough. I'll tell her. And her name is Patricia!"

"I know," Corbin said, with a slight laugh. "Have fun!"

Ben called Patricia. It was after 7:00 p.m., and they had agreed to meet at the club around 7:30 p.m.

"Hi. I just dropped off Michelle at JoAnn's and am heading to the club."

"OK, I'll be there on time."

Ben and Patricia settled into a quiet dinner of swordfish and the trimmings, with a nice white wine. It was very pleasant and they were pretty much in their own zone, when her phone rang.

"I better get this, it's JoAnn."

She took the call and all of the color left her face.

Ben was shocked. "What is it? What's happened?"

"That was Arthur—Henry's brother and JoAnn's husband."

He said that the private plane that Henry was on has disappeared off the radar and that the pilot isn't responding to the tower. Arthur is heading to the airport and will keep me informed."

She covered her mouth, and said, "Oh my gosh! Ben, what should I do?"

"Well, there isn't much that you can do at this time. If it were a commercial plane they would have a gathering place for the families and information would be provided there. I believe it would be best if you wait for an update from Arthur. Unless, of course, you feel the need to be at the airport."

"No, I think I better pick up Michelle and get home. Let me call JoAnn."

"Hi honey," JoAnn said, "are you coming over here?"

"Yes. I'm at the club having dinner with Ben, so I'll come over there now."

"Tell Ben that he is welcome to come over too."

"Ok, thanks."

"Would you like to go to JoAnn's with me?"

"Sure, if you want me to."

"I do!"

"Ok then, let's go. I'll follow you."

Michelle was asleep and JoAnn was on the phone when they arrived. She hung up. "That was Arthur. There is no updated information yet."

She opened a bottle of wine and they all had a glass.

"Are you ok, Patricia?"

"Yeah, I'm a bit numb and in disbelief. I just wonder what could have happened to that plane."

"What do you think, Ben?" JoAnn asked.

"Well, it could be several things, some good and some bad. The plane's communications could have gone out and they would still have control of the plane. Or, the pilot may have had a medical situation. Sometimes the smaller planes don't have a co-pilot. They may have been forced to land somewhere. We'll just have to wait for more input from Arthur—he's where the information will be coming in first."

Ben stepped outside on the patio and called Corbin.

"Yeah, Ben?"

"I just wanted to let you know that I might not be home anytime soon."

"Yeah, I thought you might be delayed, with that aircraft missing and all."

"You know?"

"That plane is registered to one of our targets in Chicago, Title One."

"Really! I wonder what Henry Morgan was doing on a plane owned by Title One."

"Not sure," Corbin said, "we haven't done a thorough background on Henry Morgan yet. We got his name from financial tracking data that Florence provided. We know that he is in the real estate investment business, so that fits in with what Title One does."

"Ah, that's good to know."

"At this point," Corbin said, "there isn't anything that ties Henry to their money laundering, but he has been dealing with some pretty shady characters."

"For now, I'll just keep that to myself. I don't want to hurt his wife anymore at this point. She is going through some pretty rough stuff."

"Agreed. It's about GO time in Arizona now."

"Yeah, I hope Barney and his guys are successful and come home safe."

"Me too! I wish I were there to help."

"Me too."

Ben went back inside and poured another glass of wine. The girls were focused on the television. The missing plane has become national news and the talking heads were desperately trying to outdo each other, with none of them having any new information.

The house phone rang, JoAnn jumped up to answer it.

"Hello! Oh! Hi honey, any news?"

She was quiet, listening intently; her face was solemn and her eyes were becoming wet.

Finally, she said, "Ok, I'll let her know. Thanks. Will you be home soon?"

"Oh, ok, I understand. Ok, then, be safe."

JoAnn started to softly cry. She hugged Patricia and said, "I'm so sorry, they have determined that the plane crashed in Tennessee."

Arthur said that the company that owns the plane, Title One, has a team heading to the crash site and that they will provide more information after they have assessed the situation."

Ben said, "They will have the NTSB crawling up their butt when they get there. Their representatives are usually at a crash site within three or four hours."

It was surprising, but Patricia didn't feel the need to cry. She just took her wine and sat down in front of the television, deeply involved in the reporting.

Ben went over and sat next to her. No one spoke.

Patricia thought, *HENRY IS DEAD! I HAVE TO GET THINGS ORGANIZED.*

Ben thought, *What the hell was Henry doing on that plane?*

CHAPTER SIXTEEN

Ben's phone rang at 1:00 a.m. It was Corbin,

"Yeah, what's up?"

"Hold onto your hat! I Just got a call from Florence. The raid went down about an hour and a half ago. They were able to get control and now have 7 prisoners, neutralized 10, took down a helicopter and have about 500 pounds of heroin. And a big bonus! About 200 pounds of fentanyl!

"The bad news, Barney lost two and has three others heading to the hospital. The damn helicopter had a Gatling gun onboard, but one of Barney's guys took it down with a grenade launcher."

"Must have been a real shit show!"

"Ah, the good old days!" Corbin said.

"Where did you serve?" Ben asked.

"I spent a little over two years in the sandbox tracking down highly valued targets for interrogation."

"Glad you got home safe."

"Yeah, my wife and I are too!"

"Hey Ben, are you planning on bedding down at home? There is a possibility that the problem will spread over the next 24 to 48 hours. With the loss of such a massive load of product, they might hit back just for a show of force."

"Yeah, Barney and I were thinking the same thing. I believe that I should be at my house if anything happens. I have some pretty heavy firepower there and I don't want to have Patricia in harm's way."

"Good idea," Corbin said, "I have two guys there now and will be beefing it up as time goes on. I'll tell them that you will be there and will be the commander on site. You are the only target that we are aware of in the Atlanta area."

"Ok, Corbin, Thanks again, and stay in contact."

"Will do!"

Patricia was asleep on the couch. Michelle was still upstairs in bed and JoAnn had apparently gone to bed. Ben woke Patricia softly with a kiss on the cheek. She opened her eyes but didn't move. Ben whispered, "I have to leave now but I will see you in the morning."

She shook her head ok, and he kissed her lightly on the lips. She responded, reached up, put her arm around his neck, and said, "I love you."

"I love you too, sweetie. Good night."

"Good night" she said, moving her arm and closing her eyes and said, "Call me."

"I will."

Ben went home and checked the house thoroughly. He set up a weapon at each entrance. In his bedroom he set his 12-gauge shotgun close to his bed and his 9mm on the table next to his side of the bed. He locked his bedroom door, took a shower, and went to bed. It was 3:00 a.m.

At 7:00 a.m., Ben's phone rang, it was Corbin.

"Hello, my shadow."

"Good morning, sleepyhead. How about some coffee, there are three of us, and it has been a long night."

"Ah, man! You bet."

"I'll open the front door and get the coffee going. You guys come on into the kitchen."

"Sounds good."

Corbin and his team of two came in, took off their night gear, and settled at the kitchen table. The coffee was ready and everyone was ready for something to eat.

Ben poured everyone some OJ, then fired up the stove and made some egg, onion, and mushroom omelets, sliced a couple of tomatoes and made a pile of toast. The kitchen smelled like a gourmet restaurant.

They all ate like there was no tomorrow; all talking at the same time. The main topic was the raid.

Corbin said, "We haven't seen a Gatling gun used stateside, so those guys were from across the border."

"Well, I'm so glad to be able to meet all of you," Ben said.

The other two guys were from Florida, "Boomer" and "Tank." They didn't offer their real names and that was ok.

In total, Corbin had eight special ops guys with him on this run.

Handyman (RV Combat Commander), Shark, and Bear were heading to Ben's house in a special ops RV bus.

The other three (Eagle Eye, Barbie, and Stump) were checking out Henry's home and office. They picked up his computers, phones, thumb drives, and any other electronic devices they could find.

Corbin said that Barney had directed them to determine what Henry's involvement was with Title One.

"Ben, how well did you know Henry Morgan?"

"Not at all. I met him once for a few minutes. He wasn't too friendly. But at the time, I was in his house with his wife when he arrived home." Ben smiled.

"Tomorrow we should have some details on the crash. Then we can start putting together some info on Title One," said Corbin.

"I hope so," Ben said, "I would like to help Patricia through this if I can. But I have to head out to the Caymans Monday for a Tuesday meeting."

Corbin said, "I suppose she will have lots of family around her for the next week or so."

"Yeah, that's probably true."

"Well, I better head out," Corbin said. "I need to get some guys started on digging through the data retrieved from Henry's house and office.

CHAPTER SEVENTEEN

At 7:00 a.m. the next morning Ben's alarm went off. He was startled for a few seconds until he got his focus.

He checked out the window and didn't see anyone around the back of the house.

He called Corbin. "Hello, sleepyhead. Do you always sleep in?"

"Yeah, most of the time," Ben said. "You guys ready for coffee?"

"You bet."

Ben unlocked the front door and cracked it, then headed to the kitchen to get the coffee going.

Corbin and three others came in.

"Damn!" said Ben, "You got the whole army with you."

"I don't want to be short-handed if something kicks off here."

The three guys were in combat-ready uniforms.

"Well, I know Boomer and Tank. Who are you others?"

"Eagle Eye," said the third guy, he reached out and shook Ben's hand.

"Have some coffee. I'm sorry to be the cause of your all-nighter."

"No sweat," Eagle Eye said. "We gotta be someplace! Makes us happy!"

Ben laughed softly, "Well, I do greatly appreciate it."

He turned to Corbin and said, "Was there any movement last night?"

"Nope, nothing that we could detect. But experience tells us that the longer they take to plan something, the worse it could be. I will have my full team here for the next three days. They will bring a combat-ready RV bus and park it a block or so away. The bus is fully equipped, including a launcher."

"Sounds like a plan. You know that I will be leaving for the Caymans on Monday afternoon."

"Yeah," Corbin said, "but we have two long nights before then."

"Well, schedule me for one of the shifts," Ben said.

"You can take the evening shift 1700. to 2400 tonight.(military time use by all combat teams) You will have Boomer and Tank with you. The support bus will have a combat commander, Handyman, and he will coordinate with you, should something go down during your watch."

"Roger that. Are we still using STONE MOUNTAIN?"

"Yes, throughout the operation," said Corbin.

"Great, well, you have the run of the house—sleep, food, or anything else. I need to identify the location of weapons for you, just in case."

Corbin nodded and everyone followed Ben for a sweep of the house.

At 10:15 p.m., Ben called Patricia at JoAnn's house.

"Hi, Ben, are you coming over?" Patricia asked.

"Yes, whenever you're ready."

"Come on over anytime."

"Ok, I should be there around 11:30 p.m."

Patricia poured some coffee and thought: *Oh my, there are so many things to take care of immediately. I don't know where to start! I need to get home and work out a To-Do list. – I guess I don't need the other To-Do list for Sara now. Wow! Things have really changed fast!*

Around 11:15 p.m., Ben told Corbin that he would be going to Arthur Morgan's house to visit with Patricia for a while, then he would be coming back before his shift time.

Patricia met him at the door, hugged him tightly, kissed him, and said, "Oh, Ben!" She held on for a minute or so. He wrapped his arms around her and held her tight, kissing her on the cheek, forehead, and lightly on the neck, then on the lips. They embraced for a minute or two then went inside.

JoAnn wasn't there; she had left with Michelle for some breakfast; then on to a friend's house to stay the day. They were trying to keep the news from Michelle until the time was right.

"Would you like some coffee?"

"Yeah, that would be great. How are you feeling, sweetie?"

"Still in disbelief. Do you think that they will find him, Ben?"

"I would expect so. But it depends on how complex the terrain is and how high up they are. The NTSB is extremely experienced in getting to crash sites and evaluating the scene."

"Oh, sure," she said, "I had a cousin that went to work with them in DC, right out of law school."

"We can anticipate a preliminary report within six hours from their arrival on site. It won't go out to the public, but it will go out to law enforcement and some specific government agencies. I should be able to get a copy."

"What will the report tell us?"

"Actually, not much. They will verify the number of passengers on board and some details as to their location in the plane or surrounding area. They will get the black box; the recorder that was active when the plane went down, and some general observation of the cockpit gauges."

Ben continued, "They will eventually take the complete plane back to some acceptable location to try to reconstruct it and figure out what happened."

"When can I expect them to transport Henry's body back home?"

"Oh, that will be a top priority. It should be back tomorrow or the next day. But they won't release it until they have reviewed it and maybe even done an autopsy."

"How do you know all this, Ben?"

"I was with the Texas Highway Patrol for a long time and was involved in several crashes—aircraft and trains mainly. It's never a pretty site."

He walked over to her and put his arm around her, "Do you think that you will be ok for a while?"

"I suppose that I'm in shock, because I really don't have any particular sadness or heartache. I'm kind of waiting for it to set in."

"As you know, everyone reacts to tragedies in different ways." He kissed her and said, "I need to get home and work on some paperwork for my trip."

"Oh, that's right, you're heading to the Caymans."

"Yeah, I have a meeting on Tuesday morning, so I need to go down Monday afternoon and get settled in and have a pre-visit with the person with whom I'm visiting."

"Will I see you tonight or tomorrow?"

"Not tonight. There are some guys at my house that I have to visit with this evening. But I'm sure that we can get together tomorrow. But you call me if you need me or want to talk."

"I will."

He kissed her again and she hugged him tight.

"Ben, be careful."

"I will."

Corbin was having a sandwich. It was a little after 2:00 p.m., and Ben joined him.

"Any action?" Ben asked.

"Nope, all is still on the home front."

"Did your bus get here?"

"No, it should be here around 1700."

"Boomer and Tank are upstairs doing watch duty on each side of the house, taking turns napping until you and they take over the evening shift."

"Where's Eagle Eye?"

"He's on top of the house. He's the best sniper I've ever seen. If it's within 500 yards, he can shoot a flea off your ass. And a man, at half a mile at best, should say his prayer."

"What's the longest sniper shot that you have heard of?"

"Oh, around three-fourths of a mile by some Canadian in Iraq. He was something!"

A radio squawked, "Hawk, this is Handyman."

"Go ahead," Corbin said.

"I have an ETA of 1645. Where do you want me to station?"

"Roger. Pick a spot that you can have a clear shot for at least half a block either way from the front of the house."

"Roger."

Corbin turned to Ben, "The RV will be ready for your shift. They will be set up and ready to rock within 30 minutes after arrival."

"Sounds like a well-oiled machine!"

"You can't be too ready."

"I'm going upstairs to my office to work a couple of hours on my trip. If you need me, just hit the intercom."

"Copy that."

Ben worked for a couple of hours and decided to take a shower. Then he dressed in jeans, hiking boots, and a black tee-shirt, and went to the kitchen where three guys were having coffee. Two of them he didn't know; they were obviously from the RV. They stood up and introduced themselves.

"Handyman."

"Glad to meet you, Handyman"

"Shark," another one said. They shook hands.

"Bear," the last one said. And they shook hands.

After the introductions, everyone settled back down to what they were talking about.

Then two others came in the front door. Ben walked over to meet them. "Hi, I'm Ben."

"Barbie," she said. (He didn't realize that it was a gal at first, with all the combat gear she was wearing.)

"Stump," the other one said.

"Welcome, everyone." Ben thought, *I would hate to meet this gal in a dark alley! She is as big as old Stump.*

Ben got a cup of coffee and slid into a chair at the table with them.

Stump said, "So I will double back behind the second house from here."

"Correct," Corbin said. "Because the center of firing will be at the front of the house; so, you and Barbie need to come in from the back."

"Got it."

"Ben will have operational command for the Basic Operational Support (BOS) starting at 1700, and I will relieve him at 2400.

"The BOS will be Boomer and Tank with Ben on the inside of the house, including the support for Bear and Eagle Eye. Eagle Eye will be stationed on top of the house for a clear shot in any direction.

Corbin looked at Ben and said, "You ready, cowboy?"

Ben smiled and said, "Bring it on!"

"Our best guess is that if anything happens, it will happen after midnight tonight.

We have a launcher onboard RV1. Any heavy-duty vehicle, regardless of size, will be destroyed immediately.

"That action alone should disorient them enough for us to activate our attack from three fronts," Corbin concluded.

Ben said, "I plan to be at the upstairs front window. I will be able to see the street. Boomer will be at the right-side window upstairs, in one of the bedrooms, and Tank will be at the left-side window upstairs. From there, we will be able to report to Bear and Handyman any movement on the street or in adjacent properties."

"Excellent," said Corbin.

"Who has the radios?" Ben asked.

Corbin said. "Bear, would you get Ben a radio?"

"Will do."

Ben said, "You guys have anything to eat?"

"Not yet," Stump said.

"Let me order some pizza," Ben said.

Corbin said, "The RV has a full kitchen, but pizza sounds great!"

It was 2100 hours, and everyone at all locations were chomping down on pizza and Pepsi. Ben, Boomer, and Tank had already settled into their upstairs observation stations.

At 2200, everyone else went to their assigned battle stations.

The stage was set.

Corbin (Hawk) lead commander, outside the house.

BOS (Basic Operational Support) Cowboy (Ben), Boomer, and Tank inside the house.

Bear (outside commander), Barbie, and Stump were outside around the perimeter of the house.

Handyman, the RV Commander and Shark, the heavy weapon operator were in RV1.

RV1 parked one block away to the left.

Eagle Eye (sniper) was on top of the house.

Every 15 minutes the three team leaders plus the sniper: Cowboy; Bear; Handyman; and Eagle Eye reported in to Corbin (Hawk).

At 0030 Hawk (Corbin), said into the radio, "Report status."

"Cowboy, clear."

"Bear, clear."

"Handyman, clear."

"Eagle Eye, clear."

Hawk said, "Roger, all."

At 0040 Boomer, from his right side window location reported, "Movement right, incoming."

Corbin had just made it up to Ben's location to relieve him.

He said, "Hawk, Roger."

He said to Ben, "The direction is relative to looking out of your front door. So, it would be down the street to the right and closing."

Also, a "standard" is a sedan car.

A "zip gun" is a bazooka.

A "pea shooter" is a land-to-air light missile launcher.

"Got it," Ben said.

"Ben, are you ok staying on position for now?"

"Affirmative."

"Great. Then I'll focus on the outside."

He said into the radio, "Hold your positions."

"Cowboy, Roger."

"Bear, Roger."

"Handyman, Roger.

"Eagle Eye, Roger."

"Hawk to Bear, give me size."

"Two standard packing eight."

Hawk, "Roger."

Corbin said, "Handyman, are you ready?"

Handyman, "Affirmative."

Hawk, "Ready your pea shooter toward the right, expect a bird."

Handyman, "Roger, standing by."

"Bear to Hawk, Go?"

Hawk, "Go!"

"Second standard showing a zip gun."

"Roger, Bear."

Hawk, "Eagle Eye you got eyes on second standard?"

"Roger, Hawk, ready to go."

Hawk, "Take him out."

Within 10 seconds, Eagle Eye locked in on the target and shot the man with the bazooka in the head. The bazooka fell out of the car and into the street.

Eagle Eye, "Target neutralized."

Hawk, "Roger."

All bets were off!

The men from the first car emptied out.

Eagle Eye took one out, then another one.

The other two made it to the house second down from Ben's house.

When the action started, Barbie and Stump moved around the house on the right to engage the two men out of the first car.

Barbie shot one and the second one lay down as a prisoner. She quickly bound him and tied him to a tree. Stump smacked him with his rifle, knocking him out.

Hawk this is Bear, "All targets accounted for."

Hawk, "Roger."

"Barbie, Stump, relocate to left side and hold your position."

Barbie, "Roger."

Stump, "Roger."

Cowboy, "Hawk, I will relocate to lower level to support front."

Hawk, "Roger."

Ben went down to the front door area and stationed himself in a position so he had clear vision up and down the street.

Everyone held their position, waiting for instructions from Hawk.

The second car backed up a block or so and turned around and drove out of harm's way.

Cowboy, "Stump, can you secure that zip gun?"

"Roger," Stump raced out and moved the zip gun from the street into a grassy area next to Ben's house and disarmed it.

Stump, "Zip gun secure."

Cowboy, "Roger."

Hawk, "Hold your positions."

Cowboy. "Roger."

Bear, "Roger."

Handyman, "Roger."

Eagle Eye, "Roger."

Corbin moved to Ben's location downstairs and said, "They most likely will bring in something a little heaver to try to dislodge us from the house. Or they might just attack the house. So be ready to evacuate by the back door."

"Roger," Ben said.

Everything was quiet for about 30 minutes. Then the sound of a helicopter was heard.

Hawk, "Anyone got eyes on the bird?"

Eagle Eye, "Affirmative, it's closing at about one o'clock, one mile."

Hawk, "Handyman, prepare pea shooter."

Handyman, "Roger."

Corbin turned to Ben and said, "Your neighborhood is about to get messy."

Handyman to Hawk, "We're ready for launch."

Hawk, "Roger. Launch when ready."

Handyman. "Roger."

The helicopter came over the treetop directly toward the front of Ben's house and RV1 fired its missile, hitting the helicopter's center mass.

The helicopter veered to its left and just missed the house two doors down on the right, landing in a deep drainage ditch. The explosion was massive, lighting up the whole neighborhood and making a loud BOOM!

The fuel ran down the drainage ditch, on fire, looking like the lava from a volcano.

Hawk, "REPORT STATUS and hold your positions."

Cowboy, "Roger, all clear."

Bear, "Roger, all clear."

Handyman, "Roger, all clear."

Eagle Eye, "Roger, all clear."

Within 30 minutes the fire trucks arrived, and then the locals.

Ben became the front guy and reported everything to all who mattered and promised a thorough report, as it will be reported to the AG of Georgia, the DEA, the FBI, and U.S. Justice Department.

All seemed to be satisfied.

After a couple of hours, Corbin called an "all clear."

He directed Eagle Eye to maintain watch from his position on top of the house.

All other team members were released from their battle stations. But all were in standby mode with weapons.

Stump retrieved the bazooka and took it to the RV for storage.

Barbie took her prisoner to the RV and secured him.

Corbin and Ben went down to the kitchen for a cup of coffee.

"I doubt if they will be coming back," Corbin said. "I'm sure that they were not expecting such a massive response. They will regroup in Mexico and work on making up the losses."

Ben said, "I would bet that they change their distribution contact locations from Arizona to some other border state."

"Yeah," Corbin said, laughing, "like Texas!"

"Yep, that would be my guess too."

It was after 4:00 a.m., and everyone was relaxed and having coffee, laughing and rehashing the action. Ben had never seen such enjoyment shown after a massive fight like that. They started working on the RV guys, trying to get them to cook up some breakfast.

Corbin said to Ben, "We will stay another day then go back to just four—me and three others—for a few more days."

"Well, obviously the house is yours as long as you are here."

"Thanks!"

"Thanks for the support! Great job to everyone! I assume that you will be providing a full report?"

"Yes, to Florence and Barney within a couple of hours. With a copy to you."

"Ok, thanks, and good night!" He went to his room and fell into bed.

CHAPTER EIGHTEEN

It was 10:00 a.m. Monday morning. The sun was shining and everything was quiet, as it should be in a peaceful neighborhood in America.

Ben got up, showered, shaved, and dressed for a summer day!

Corbin received word from Barney to clear out of Ben's house and retreat to their home base. So, the house was empty and clear. The cleaning crew was coming in soon to convert the house back into livable shape.

Ben got his paper and coffee and settled into his favorite chair. The headlines were still full of the attack and military type battle that went on in a quiet community just outside of Atlanta.

He chuckled at some of the off-base comments made by reporters that had never been to his neighborhood and most likely never been in any area where there had been a major military battle.

He smiled and thought, It's all about selling papers!

Ben's flight to the Caymans was scheduled for 1:00 p.m. It was a two-and-a-half-hour flight with a time zone loss of one hour. The ETA was around 5:00 p.m., leaving enough time for him to get to his hotel and freshen up before meeting Ms. Beatrice Farmer.

Ben called Ms. Farmer and gave her his flight and hotel arrangements to make sure that she would be available upon his arrival.

He then called Patricia's cell.

"Good morning," Patricia said. "Are you getting ready to leave for your trip?"

"Yes, but I wanted to come by to see you before I leave."

"Great!"

Ben said "Are you home?"

"No. I'm still at JoAnn's."

"Ok, I'll see you in a few minutes."

He dressed and carried his bag to the car, and drove over to see Patricia. She met him at the door. They kissed and smiled lovingly. and went inside to sit in the kitchen.

"When is your flight?"

"1:00 p.m."

"Wow, you're already late!"

"Nah, I generally get to the airport an hour or so ahead of departure. I have a special ID that gets me through the lines and allows me to carry a weapon. So, I'm good."

"So, you're special!" she laughed.

He laughed with her and said, "No! YOU are special! And I'll miss you for the next few days."

"When will you be back?"

"I'm planning on Thursday."

"Good! I will really miss you—and I need you."

"You can call me anytime. When will your family be coming in?"

"Tomorrow, I think. Dad has a private plane, so he'll pick up some of the family along the way."

"Ah, that's good. I'll be thinking of you, my dear, and remember to call if you need to talk."

"I will."

They talked a little about the accident and she shared with him that Henry's body had been returned and was being held by the government for now. She asked if he had seen a report on the crash.

"No, not yet."

She asked about the attack on his house. "The blast was very loud and we could see the action from here!"

"Sorry about that," Ben said, with a smile.

Ben looked at his watch and it was time to leave. They walked to the door, she kissed him, her passion was obvious as she held him close.

"I'll be waiting for you when you come home."

"Good to know," he said, with a smile. He kissed her again and walked to the car. They waved goodbye and she went inside.

When Patricia returned home from JoAnn's, it was a shock to find the house in disarray. It had been invaded and things had been taken.

As Corbin had told Ben, his team had been there and took Henry's computer and other items relating to electronic communication and storage. The team left Patricia a report on all that had been taken and where it was being taken. And that it would be returned once the investigation was complete. A phone number that she could call, if she had any questions was also included.

But they had not found the private business computer and files relating to his job. They were all concealed behind a fake wall in the guestroom closet which she knew about.

Patricia realized that someone was checking on Henry's business.

She called Ben.

"Hi there, what's up?"

"Hi, do you know anything about Henry being suspected of anything?"

"No, why?"

"Well, when I got home it was obvious that someone had been in the house and had taken things from Henry's office. His computer, files, and other things were missing."

"Well, According to the guy that I've been working with, Henry was on a plane owned by a company that the government is investigating. Maybe they are just trying to put together the puzzle. But, to my knowledge, no one is accusing Henry of any wrong doings at this time."

"Ok. Would you tell me if they were?"

"If it happens, and I'm allowed to share that information, I will. But you have to remember; I'm on the government's side in this deal. And most of it is highly confidential."

"I realize and respect that Ben, but I'm getting scared, not knowing what's going on."

"Yes, I can see that, and I will be here to support you."

"Ok, thank you. See you in a few days. I love you."

"Love you too, and take care of yourself."

Patricia wasn't sure what to do. She didn't really know how important the information was, but she knew that Henry had stashed away a considerable amount of money for emergencies. She would have to try to figure it all out. Then decide what to do.

CHAPTER NINETEEN

Ben arrived on Grand Cayman, Owen Roberts International, at 5:10 p.m. local time. The flight was a little late departing Atlanta, but made up some of the time in the air. Ben hailed a cab and went to his hotel, Turtle Nest Inn, Room 430. He checked in, checked out his room, hung up his clothes, stored his bag, and then called the desk.

"Yes, Mr. Berkshire, how may I help you?"

"I was hoping you might refer me to a good restaurant."

"Of course, sir. Are you thinking about seafood?"

"Yes."

"Ok, I believe that you would be satisfied at the Hard Rock Café. It comes highly recommended by many guests."

"How far is it from here?"

"Not very far; maybe nine miles. I can have someone take you there and pick you up. What time would you like to dine?"

"7:30 p.m. would be great."

"Very well sir, I will make your reservations and call with a reminder at 7:15."

"Thank you."

"You are so welcome. And have a wonderful stay."

It was 5:55 p.m. Ben got a cold beer out of the bar area and took it and his briefcase outside on the balcony and sat down.

He leaned back and closed his eyes, enjoying the relaxed environment. The soft, salty breeze took hold of his mind. His thoughts filled with the unbelievable combat action that took place right in his neighborhood. Then his thoughts shifted to Patricia.

He was very confused about exactly where they were and what steps he should take toward a closer relationship with her. He still wasn't totally comfortable.

He made a note to call Corbin about a preliminary report on the plane crash, and another note to call Barney to see if there was any chatter on the wires that would indicate where the distributors would be moving their port of entry.

He sat back in his chair and suddenly his phone rang. He jumped! He had fallen asleep.

The call was his advance notice for the trip to the restaurant. He thanked the desk clerk and went down to the front to wait for his ride. On the way, he called Ms. Farmer to let her know that he was on the island, and invited her for a drink and/or dinner at the restaurant.

She declined the offer and said that she would look forward to meeting him in her office around 9:00 a.m. the following day.

Ben had a house salad with oil and vinegar and fried oysters and a baked potato with lots of butter. The meal was excellent and so was the service. He paid the bill and a healthy tip and called the hotel for transportation.

The ride was there in 15 minutes.

Ben thanked the desk clerk for the very enjoyable restaurant recommendation and gave her a ten-dollar bill.

A little after 9:00 p.m. Corbin called.

"Hi," Ben said, "To what do I owe the pleasure?"

"Well, first, you can sit down!"

"Oh?"

"Yep, another big surprise. This case just gets more squirrely by the hour. We got the NTSB preliminary report on the site search. The plane was intact; except there was one engine about 200 yards away from the site. Most likely hit a tree coming down. But the most significant notation was that only one body was onboard—that being Mr. Henry Morgan. And, a thorough search showed only two parachutes onboard. On that aircraft there are normally four."

"So, as you, a seasoned investigator, would surmise, a couple of people deplaned prior to impact."

"Your thoughts?" Corbin asked.

"Interesting. My next question would be to the coroner, to find out just how Mr. Morgan died. My bet would be either a gunshot or blunt force trauma."

"See! My exact thoughts! That's the reason I like working with you—you're so logical. I'll call the coroner first thing in the morning and get back to you."

"Now assuming that we are on target," Ben said, "don't you think that puts our Mr. Morgan in the thick of things in Chicago?"

"For sure. Yes, for sure."

"Thanks, Corbin. Please let me know what you find out."

"Will do."

Ben hung up the phone and got a beer from the refrigerator and went out on the balcony. A delightful sea breeze was blowing and there were lighted cabanas along the shore with service personnel moving about. It was such a relaxing place.

He thought *Maybe it would be a great place to bring Patricia for a short vacation after all of this settles down.*

Then his thoughts drifted back to the report that Corbin shared. *Could Henry really be a part of the laundering business? And if he was, did Arthur or JoAnn or even Patricia know about it?*

There were so many questions.

He sat in a large soft lounge chair and drifted off to sleep.

A little after 11:00 p.m., Ben's phone rang.

It was Patricia. "I hope I didn't wake you."

"Actually, you did and I appreciate it. I fell asleep on a lounge chair on the balcony just outside my room."

She laughed. "Now that's being relaxed!"

"I suppose so. Is everything ok?"

"Oh yes, I was just thinking about you and wanted to hear your voice before I retire for the night."

"Well, that was mighty sweet. Thanks."

"I have a meeting at 9:00 a.m. in the morning, so I need to get in bed too."

"By the way, I got a call from my guy about the site report. He said that he would have something in the morning."

"So, after my meeting and most likely lunch, I'll check with him. I'll let you know one way or the other."

"Ok, great, thanks. We will be having a memorial service for Henry on Wednesday. When they are finished with his body he will be cremated and, as he had requested, the ashes will be spread in New York Harbor."

"Ok, I'm sorry that I won't be there to support you."

"To tell you the truth, this place will be crawling with family for two days. So, I'll really need you when you get back—just you and me."

"Sounds good. Good night."

"Good night, I love you."

"Love you too."

He had decided not to give her any information until it was complete. Also, he was hoping that Corbin would have something from all the equipment that they took out of Henry's house.

He hated to admit it, but he had to assume that Patricia had to know something about Henry's business relationship with Title One. *Damn! He thought, why does this have to happen this way?*

He took a shower and jumped into bed, asleep in a very short while.

CHAPTER TWENTY

Ben's 7:00 a.m. wakeup call rang.

He did not wake up once throughout the night. The door to the balcony had been left ajar and the soft sea breeze made sleeping a dream.

He called room service and ordered coffee and lay in bed watching the news until it arrived.

The private plane crash in Tennessee was a hot topic. But nothing new was available. The NTSB had not released any information regarding the fact that only one person had been found at the crash site. They just said that the investigation is still ongoing.

The coffee came and the waitperson placed it on the table on the balcony. He gave her five bucks and settled into the chair at the table. She had left a Houston paper with the coffee. He flipped through it looking for anything that would shed light on their case.

Nothing!

He went inside and shaved and dressed. Since he was on the island, he decided to dress the part. He put on a pair of white slacks and an aloha shirt. He smiled at himself in the mirror and thought, *There aren't many places you can get away with this kind of attire!*

He went down to the dining room for a quick bite. He sat down and picked up the menu.

Someone bumped into his elbow, kind of forcefully. Looking up, he saw, a tall, strong-looking young man of about 30, looking down at him.

The guy said, "I think I know you. Have you been to STONE MOUNTAIN?"

Ben almost fell out of his chair! "Yes, I have been there. But I'm not sure that I know you."

"Corbin sent me. I'm Handyman."

Ben didn't recognize Handyman without all of his combat gear!

"Have a seat, Handyman." They sat across from each other looking at menus.

Without dropping the menu to look at him, Ben said, "What's the occasion?"

"Security risk," Handyman said, also not lowering his menu.

"You were RV1 Commander, right?"

"Good memory."

"There has been significant chatter on the wire, indicating the desire to track you down. So, Corbin decided to send me down until you return to Atlanta. I've checked in here last night." He laughed slightly. "I slept on your balcony for a few hours last night."

Ben laughed too. "You guys are really something. I really do appreciate your help. Is the security a part of your team, or just local?"

"All team members."

"I just talked with Corbin last night."

"I know. He couldn't comment while talking on the open wires, and I was already on site."

"Well, let's have some breakfast; I have a 9:00 a.m. meeting, as you most likely already know."

"Yes."

Both men had scrambled eggs, bacon, toast, and OJ.

At 8:30 a.m., Ben paid the bill and got up to leave.

"I have a car out front. I'll drive you and pick you up. Do you have a weapon?"

"Yes."

"Ok, I have another 9mm in the car, if you need it."

"Ok, thanks."

They drove to Cayman National Bank to meet Ms. Farmer. Handyman remained outside with the car.

Ms. Farmer was a physically fit lady of forty-something; hard to tell because she seemed to be in such great shape.

Ben introduced himself and shook her hand. If you didn't know better, you would think that you were shaking the hands of a boxer—so strong and controlling. She had a cropped hair style and her face seem to glow, and the twinkle in her eyes made you feel that you were friends.

"Please have a seat. It's not often that I receive a new guest down here. While the island is lovely and relaxing, you do get 'island fever' every now and then."

"Where do you go for relief?"

"Oh, I fly over to Las Vegas or Houston, I have an off-shore banking meeting a few times a year, and I get up to Washington D.C. every few weeks."

"Well, it sounds like you are a busy lady."

"Yeah, there's always something going on to focus on. So, Mr. Berkshire, what brings you to our beautiful paradise?"

"I'm working with a client that has need of some private and secure cash deposits. But he desires that they remain confidential."

"We are in that business, as are many other banks on the island. What made you decide on National?"

"The bank—and especially you—come highly recommended. A long-time friend of mine in Houston referred me to you. A Mr. Frank Keith."

"Of course, I know Mr. Keith."

She picked up a packet and handed it to him and said, "I believe that you will find everything in here that you need to establish a business relationship with us."

And she handed him one of her business cards. It had some writing on the back. "I will meet you at 11:30 a.m. at Andiamo's. It's just past the Ritz-Carlton Hotel. After you have completed the necessary paperwork, just send it to me or, if you are still on the island, you may drop it at my office."

She stood, as did he, they shook hands and looked closely at each other, and Ben departed. It was 9:30 a.m.

Outside, Handyman was waiting with the engine running. They drove down to the beach. Ben had not said anything and neither had Handyman.

Ben finally spoke, "I got the feeling that that lady is working in a dangerous environment. And that she is very capable of taking care of herself. We will meet her in a couple of hours at Andiamo's. I'm not sure of the directions, but it's close to the Ritz-Carlton Hotel."

"No problem, I'll get it in a second." He made a call and jotted down an address. "Got it."

Ben took out his phone and dialed Corbin.

"Yeah, Ben."

"Hi. First, thanks for the escort. I feel a lot better with Handyman here."

"No problem. We aim to please!" He laughed.

"Is it ok if I include Handyman in my meetings? Two heads are better than one."

"You bet. He has full Top Secret security clearance."

"Great! Met Ms. Farmer at the bank and quickly became aware that our business could not be discussed there. She slipped me a note that she would meet me at Andiamo's in a couple of hours."

"Ok, then, call me if you need anything."

"Thanks!"

"You bet."

It was almost 12:00 noon when Ms. Farmer arrived. They picked a corner booth. Ben introduced Handyman and gave her some general background on how they met. He advised her that he had full security clearance.

She said, "Ok."

"Are you having any specific security issues at this time?" Ben asked.

"No, but everything and everywhere in that bank is wired—video and audio."

"Got it. What can you tell me about Island Distribution? I understand that it's a shell company for moving money from various businesses on the mainland to Mexico. Is that about it?"

"That's true, but it does a lot more than that. It moves funds to other secure banking facilities all over the world. The operation is made up of five people, four men and one woman. All from Mexico City."

"How much do they move through your bank on, say, a monthly basis?"

"Between 10 and 100 million American dollars."

"Big operation," Handyman said.

"Yes, and when they are in our bank, the manager closes the entrance to all other customers. They basically have the run of the bank. I believe that in addition to being high profile customers, the manager is very afraid of them. They roughed him up a couple of times to remind him that they were in charge. All of the other managers, including myself, stay clear when they are in the bank doing their business. I'm not afraid of them, but I can't blow my cover. We, the Justice Department have been working this case for over seven years. What is your concern with them, Ben?"

"They are a part of a group that have been moving heroin and fentanyl into the U.S. then distributing it to major cities like Seattle, L.A., Houston, and Chicago, just to name a few. They are extremely dangerous. Just a few days ago they attacked my personal home in Atlanta. But I was lucky; I had Handyman and his fantastic combat team there."

"So that was your house! Wow! What a shit show that must have been!" Ben laughed. "That's exactly what I called it!"

"Where did you serve?" Handyman asked.

"Fallujah, 82nd Airborne."

Handyman said, "Well, welcome home. I spent some time there too. Rangers."

"Yeah," she said, "Welcome home."

Ben said, "I'm so proud of you guys! What a sacrifice you made. I thank you so much for your service."

She said, "Thanks, it was our job and we were working toward a return home."

"Well, welcome home!" Ben said.

"Ms. Farmer—" She interrupted, "My friends call me Bee."

"Thanks, Bee. Is there any tangible recorded information that I can tie back to any of the real estate operations working in Chicago or Seattle, to start with? The companies are Title One in Chicago and Multiple Family Investing, in Seattle. There are others, but these seem to be handling a large quantity of the funds."

"I will call you tomorrow, Ben, for another meeting."

They had lunch and some laughs about stories of the "good old days," mainly Bee's and Handyman's war stories. It was great laughing and talking as old friends.

After a couple of hours Bee departed, back to work. Ben and Handyman went down the beach to check out some of the local spots. A little free time.

A little after 5:00 p.m., Ben received a call from Corbin. The coroner had completed his examination of Mr. Morgan. As suspected, he died from a blunt force trauma. His skull was crushed from behind.

"So," Corbin said, "I suspect he must have become a liability for the operation. Maybe talked too much, or even expressed a desire to get out. Who knows? But one thing's for sure, they became very unhappy with him."

"Too bad. That will be tough news for Patricia."

"And now, we have to take a close look at her potential involvement."

"I know," Ben said.

Ben called Florence, shared with her the information that Bee had passed on, and told her that he would get back with her after the meeting on Wednesday.

"Do you have anyone with you, Ben?"

"Yes, Corbin sent down one of his guys, Handyman. So, we're good."

"I know him. Good man. Ok then, I'll wait for your call tomorrow—and be safe, Ben."

"Will do!"

"Everyone seems to know you," Ben said to Handyman.

"Yeah, I get around. And I've been doing this for many years, since I was 18!"

"Good to know. Let's get back to the hotel and get something to eat."

"Sounds good to me!"

"By the way, Handyman, what room are you in?"

"Just next door to yours—we share the same balcony."

"Ok."

They had a nice dinner at the hotel restaurant and talked a bit.

It was after 7:00 p.m., and Ben had a lot of paperwork to look through and wanted to prepare some meaty questions for the meeting with Bee. He called it a night, and they both went to their own room.

CHAPTER TWENTY-ONE

Wednesday morning at 6:00 a.m. Patricia woke with Michelle jumping onto her bed. Apparently, the gang—Patricia's mom, dad, aunt and her 20-year-old daughter had spent the night there, to attend the service later on that morning.

Michelle wasn't aware of why everyone was there, but she was excited to see them.

Patricia just wanted it all to be over! Then some way, somehow, she would have to tell Michelle that her dad wasn't coming home.

She got up, asked Michelle to go find Grandma while she took a shower. After she was dressed, she went downstairs to meet the horrible day.

Her mother was in the kitchen. The coffee smelled wonderful, and eggs and bacon reminded her of when she lived in a simpler, happier time. When she was a young girl, her mother always met her in the kitchen with an eye-twinkling smile, so happy to see her child. She was such a loving, caring mother.

Now, today they would be having a painful experience. Saying goodbye to a dear member of their family. As far as her mother knew.

Patricia kissed her mom on the cheek and poured two cups of coffee; one for her and one for her dad, who had just walked into the room. He was quiet and thanked her for the coffee. She kissed him on the cheek.

"Will you be able to stay another night or so?" Patricia asked.

"No," said her father. "I have so many meetings being pushed back, I have to get back to the firm. We will be leaving right after the service, and should be airborne by 1:00 p.m."

"Too bad, it's so nice having you here."

"You and Michelle should move back to New York and you could work with me," her dad said, with a loving smile. "It would be wonderful having you there."

"Ah, dad, that's so nice of you. I really appreciate the offer. But I have things to get settled here. I just might take you up on the offer one day, though."

Her mother beamed with excitement and said, "Oh, honey! That would be so great!"

"We'll see," Patricia said.

The service went well, Patricia kind of drifted through it. Her thoughts were on all that stuff hidden away in the house.

After the service, Patricia said goodbye to the family and she and JoAnn, with Michelle and Brooklyn went to the club for lunch. On the way over, Patricia asked JoAnn, "Do you know much about the business Henry and Arthur were in?"

It was obvious to Patricia that JoAnn hesitated, but then said, "There were stories around the office and with their friends about different things, but I'm personally not aware of any details of the business."

"What stories? I've never heard anything."

"Well, you wouldn't, since you haven't been a part of our parties and gatherings. Henry would come but you seemed to avoid them."

"He never told me about any parties that the company had, JoAnn! I guess he preferred to spend that time with his girlfriend."

"I don't know, Patricia, I just went when Arthur said we were going."

"What stories?" Patricia asked.

"Oh, about big paydays for special projects; and the BIG parties in Chicago with one of the company's main clients."

"Did you go to those?"

"Yeah, Arthur and I would fly up with other people in the company."

"Like Henry and his girlfriend?"

"Yes, she would be there."

"So, the stories were primarily about money?" Patricia continued to probe.

"Yes."

"Interesting!"

They had lunch, then Patricia drove home. She had a lot of things to do and to think about.

She called the company attorney, Brad Barton, "Hi Brad, this is Patricia Morgan."

"Hi Patricia, I'm so sorry for your loss."

"Thank you, Brad.

I need to know what happens to Henry's ownership and control in the company now."

"The bylaws provide for a cash settlement for Henry's wife and children."

"So, I will have no stock in the company?"

"No. The cash settlement is the means by which the company buys back Henry's stock and position."

"Oh, ok. Thanks, Brad."

"You're welcome, and, again, I'm sorry for your loss, Patricia."

"Thanks."

"Also, I will have all the required papers ready with a check, whenever you wish to take care of the settlement."

"I do appreciate that, Brad. I will be by within the next couple of days."

"Ok, good."

"Oh, by the way, exactly how much is that settlement?"

"With one child, it comes out to two million, six hundred thousand dollars."

"Thank you, Brad." They hung up.

It was 2:30 p.m., Patricia had let Michelle go home with JoAnn to play with Brooklyn, so she could have some free time to think and also to check out the stuff in the guestroom hideaway.

She got home, opened a bottle of wine, poured a glass, and went into the guestroom. She took out the computer and records from the hiding place, tossing everything on the bed. . . . and just looked at it.

There were accounting ledger books, notebooks with handwritten records and some other written information, a thumb drive, and a recorder. She first connected the computer to the wall and turned it on, but it was password protected. She smiled. Everywhere Henry used a password it had something to do with Michelle.

She tried several things, then Michelle's birthday. It worked—and the computer sprang into operation. Searching the files, she didn't see anything to do with money, banks, or investments.

She then placed the thumb drive into the slot,

BINGO!

Bank accounts, detailed routing instructions with account numbers, and pass codes.

The first bank on the list was Cayman National Bank.

She opened it and the current balance was fifteen million, three hundred thousand American dollars!

"Oh my!" she exclaimed, leaning back on the bed and laughing. She then sat up and looked again, taking a big drink of wine.

She started checking other accounts. There were three: Hong Kong, London, and the one in the Caymans. The first two accounts totaled less than one million dollars.

There was also a note to her from Henry, telling her that if anything ever happened to him, she should open an account in Zürich and transfer the funds to the new account. Also, that if there was a question about how he died, the transfer should be made immediately. He provided instructions with all the details needed to set up the account and make the transfers.

She wrote down the information, went to the kitchen, got another glass of wine, and within 20 minutes she had moved over 16 million dollars into a personal, private, secure account in a bank in Zürich.

She took the information relevant to the new account and hid it in the seam of her personal robe in her closet. She had also memorized the account number and personal password.

She replaced the computer and books and everything else except the thumb drive back into the wall and secured it as it was originally. And, with a smile, she thought, *He might have been a cheater, but he was a hell of a provider!*

She kept the thumb drive, deciding to place that in a safe place for future reference. She also made a backup copy to send to her father for storage.

It was 4:30 p.m., and she was exhausted, but exhilarated! Patricia was looking at a future with promise and no worries about money. She lay across her bed, smiling, and fell asleep.

At 8:00 p.m. Patricia woke to a phone call. It was JoAnn, "Are you planning to pick up Michelle? It's bedtime and she doesn't have clothes over here."

"Oh, I'm sorry, JoAnn, I'll be right over."

When she arrived at JoAnn's there was music and wine waiting.

"I hope you don't mind, but I put some of Brooklyn's clothes on Michelle after they both took a bath. They are upstairs playing."

"No, that's great."

Arthur was still at the office. He would now be the president of the company.

Patricia took the wine and kissed JoAnn on the cheek. "Thanks, my dear, for taking care of Michelle. It has been a day! I was asleep when you called. Just exhausted. Everyone is gone now, so maybe I can start getting things under control. There is so much to do."

"I can imagine! Just let me know if I can help."

"I will, for sure!"

"Have you thought about what you might do?"

"No, not really. Dad is trying to get me to move up there and join his firm. But, New York? I don't know."

"You once loved it, during school and those good old days!" She smiled.

"Yeah, but once we moved down south and things slowed down, I liked it here."

"Well, of course! And I would love for you to stay here. But after Henry's death, it might be too much."

"You might be right. I'll have to get things under control then make that decision."

"And what about Ben?" JoAnn asked.

"That's one of the things that has to be worked out before I can make a decision. I do love him. But, well, I just don't know."

"Have some more wine."

"Yeah! One important thing at a time."

They both laughed, and it felt good.

As Patricia thought about all the possibilities for the future, she was bubbly with excitement inside.

She had enough money to live anywhere or do anything she desired. And she just could not wait to get going on planning for her new life.

"Maybe I will just leave Michelle here with Brooklyn tonight."

"No problem."

Patricia kissed JoAnn on the cheek and said, "Thanks, I'll see you in the morning."

"Good night, my dear."

"Good night."

CHAPTER TWENTY-TWO

At 7:00 a.m., the phone rang in Ben's room. He looked at the clock and said to himself, *good morning, Handyman!*

He picked up the receiver and Handyman said, "Up and at 'em, sleepyhead."

"Ok," Ben laughed and said, "You sound like Corbin! Give me 20 minutes. I'll meet you in the coffee shop."

"Copy that."

Ben took a quick shower, shaved, and went to the coffee shop to start the day! He was hoping that Bee would be able to give them some useful information today. He wanted to get back to the mainland.

Handyman was smiling and rested after an uneventful night of sleep. "Good morning, how are you today? Did you get any sleep?"

"Yes, I slept like a baby. How about you?"

"Wonderful. Ready to fight the sharks! What's our plan for the day?"

"Well, we are waiting for a call from Bee and I'm hoping that it will be productive so we can get back to the mainland."

"Sounds good."

They ordered coffee and discussed, in general, what they hoped to accomplish. Then they ordered eggs, toast, and Handyman had bacon.

Within 30 minutes they had eaten and were ready to leave. They walked along the beach, waiting for Bee to call. At 11:00 a.m., she called and asked them to meet her at noon at Andiamo's for lunch.

"We'll be there."

Handyman said, "I think I'll grab a cab now and just head on down there to take a good look around and watch who comes and goes between now and noon."

"Great idea. Thanks."

"Just doing my job, old man." They both laughed.

Ben sat on a bench for a while, thinking about Patricia and what her involvement, if any, might be in the case; and what his relationship could be with her, given the situation. He also wanted to know what Arthur's involvement might be, since he would become the next president of the company. So many questions!

At 11:30 a.m., Ben received a call from Handyman. "There are two suspicious, local characters in a Jeep parked a block away from the restaurant. They seem to be focused on the restaurant. I'll watch the two of you come and go into the restaurant and see what these guys do, if anything."

"Roger that."

Ben met Bee at the entrance of the restaurant and they went in.

"Where's Handyman?"

"He'll be along soon." He thought, *No need to discuss the details of the potential situation.*

The two men got out of the Jeep. Handyman noticed an automatic weapon under a towel around one man's waist. He screwed a silencer onto his 9mm pistol and walked toward the two guys.

They were about 30 yards away. There was no one else in close proximity, so when he got even with them, he turned around behind them.

He said to the guy with the weapon, "Drop the weapon."

The guy started raising the weapon toward Handyman and Handyman shot him in the upper leg. The man screamed and dropped the weapon and fell to the ground.

The second man turned toward Handyman and asked, "Who are you?"

"Don't worry about who I am. Do you have a weapon?"

"Yes!"

"Take it out and drop it." The man did as he was told.

"Now, give me your wallets."

"What?" the second man said.

"I said give me your wallets. I want some identification."

They both took out their wallets and handed them over.

"Now, let's go back to your Jeep."

They all three walked back to the Jeep, the second man helping the first man that was shot.

"Both of you get into the front." They did.

He got into the back with his weapon out, pointing toward the two men.

He opened the first man's wallet; he was from Mexico City. The second man proved to be also.

Handyman dialed 911. He asked for assistance and gave the operator an international police password. Within five minutes, there were two police cars on site. One car had a detective sergeant.

Handyman spoke with the detective and briefed him on the situation on the mainland and that these two were suspected of being a part of that attack on Mr. Benjamin Berkshire's home.

The detective said, "Yes, I read about the incident. Ok, we'll take them downtown and lock them up. We'll get some medical aid for that one. And you can call your people and have them send me the necessary papers to extradite them to Atlanta."

"Sounds good. I really appreciate your help. Also, there are two weapons down on the sidewalk, belonging to these two guys."

The detective said, "Thanks."

Handyman called Corbin and gave him a briefing. Corbin said, "I'll take care of it from here. You get over to the restaurant and stay close to Ben and Bee."

"Will do."

Handyman went into the restaurant, found Ben and Bee, apologized for being late, and melted into the luncheon meeting. After they left the restaurant in a cab, Handyman gave a detailed report to Ben.

"Damn! Those guys in Mexico just can't take a joke!"

Handyman laughed. "Sure seems that way!"

"So, get any good scoop from Bee?"

"Yes and no. She was able to confirm the involvement of the two companies that we told her about, but she wasn't able to provide any detailed files or proof of their activities. However, we now know that they send money to the shell company, but for what, we don't know. Looks like we will have to get our information directly from the companies in Seattle and Chicago."

"It's getting complicated," Handyman said.

Ben laughed, "Nah, just a little bump in the road!"

Ben called Florence and gave her the info that he had received from Bee, which wasn't much. And they discussed tentative plans to go to Chicago to investigate Title One.

Ben had more than one reason to make Title One the first stop.

Handyman called Corbin and advised him that they would be leaving the island in about six hours, around 9:00 p.m. Should I stay with Ben or go back to Phoenix?"

"There's no need for you to come to Atlanta. We have plenty of support out of our office. Just go on back home."

"Roger that, I'll let Ben know."

"Ok. Good job, Handyman!"

"Thanks."

Handyman told Ben what his instructions were from Corbin. He advised Ben that it would be best if he, Ben, got a first flight out to Atlanta then he would leave, after it was safe. They agreed and went back to the hotel to make arrangements and pack.

Ben's flight left around 8:40 p.m., with a stop in Houston. Handyman flew out at 09:20 p.m., direct to Phoenix. Ben had a delay of almost an hour in Houston and lost another hour due to the time zone. By the time he got his luggage and a cab in Atlanta, it was after 3:00 a.m.

He was glad to be home! Tula was still at the Pet Hotel. So, he took a shower, turned off his phone, and fell into bed.

CHAPTER TWENTY-THREE

The alarm at 7:00 a.m. brought Ben out of a deep sleep. Being in his own bed and with no known worries of danger, he had slept like a baby. He went to the kitchen for some of *his own* home-brewed coffee and to wade through his mail.

He had told Florence that he would go to Chicago in a week or so to checkout Title One, in hopes of gathering some detailed information on their association with the shell company, Island Distribution. But, before he can leave, he has to meet with Patricia. He is genuinely concerned about her emotional condition. And he also is hoping to get a feel for her knowledge of Henry's involvement with Title One.

Henry being on Title One's plane that crashed, and him being the only casualty just couldn't mean anything but trouble. He had to be involved with their financial situation, moving money from place to place. But, did Patricia know anything about it?

He called Patricia.

"Good morning, Ben!"

Good morning, my dear, how are you this fine day?"

"I'm doing very well, thanks. Are you back in town?"

"Yes, just got in late last night. Are you available for some coffee and maybe breakfast?"

"Sure. I'm looking forward to seeing you."

"Yeah! Me, too! How about 10:00 a.m. at the club?"

"Sounds great!"

"Ok then, I'll see you there."

It was about 8:30 a.m., and Ben decided to pick up Tula at the Pet Hotel. It was only a couple of miles from the house.

She was so happy to see him! Her little tail looked like it was gonna fly off!

Ben paid the bill and picked her up. She was licking him and trying to jump around. She was such a wonderful little dog.

They started for home, Ben and Tula. But he stopped at the Dairy Queen and got a small cup of ice cream and put it on the passenger side floor. Tula loved ice cream. She went to work on it, licking and pushing it around, just having a wonderful time. By the time they got home, it was half gone! He took Tula and the ice cream into the house and placed them both on the floor in the kitchen.

Tula was in heaven!

He poured himself another cup of coffee and continued the cursory viewing of his mail. Nothing stood out as urgent. So, he took his coffee and the current day's paper and headed for his 'morning chair.'

The paper was filled with the same old political and gory stuff, so he was only reading the headlines. But on page 8 of the local section there was a small article about Henry.

The details were nothing close to being correct. But it did say that he was killed in a private plane crash en route from Chicago to Atlanta; and that his body had been found and returned to his wife who lived on Dennison Drive.

Nothing about him being the only person on the plane or anything about the number of parachutes found at the crash site. Ben assumed that the FBI had suppressed the details.

It was 9:40 a.m., so Ben left home for the club to meet Patricia, who was waiting outside at the entrance.

"Hello there!" she said, as he came up the steps.

"Hello, yourself! You are a sight for sore eyes." He took her into his arms and held her. She pulled back and kissed him passionately. She held on for a long while and then said, "Damn, I missed you!"

Ben smiled with his eyes and said, "It's really nice to see you too, sweetie."

She held onto his arm as they entered the club and went into the dining room. They settled into a nice spot overlooking the putting green. She told him about the service for Henry and about her family—who came and who didn't. He talked a little about the Cayman Island trip, but just general stuff.

They ordered OJ and pancakes. While they were eating, the conversation came to an end. Both momentarily in deep thought about what needed to be shared, and how to say it.

"Have you received any more news about the crash? Has there been a report released yet?"

"No, the report hasn't been released by the NTSB, but I did receive some classified portions of the report. The plane that Henry was traveling on was owned by Title One, a real estate investment company. That company is under investigation by the FBI. Henry's body was the only body found at the crash site, and there were indications that he had been knocked out or killed before the plane crash. Also, the evidence indicates that he was the only person onboard the plane when it crashed. It is believed that two other people left the plane while in flight."

"How would they know that?"

"Well, that type of plane carries four parachutes and there were only two found at the crash site. And, no other bodies were found."

"My gosh! Why would someone want to kill Henry?"

"I don't know. I was hoping that you might be able to shed some light on that part."

"What do you mean?"

"I don't know, maybe you might remember something that Henry said about Title One; or you might have heard something about what his business was with them?"

"I don't have any idea about any of his business deals. He never discussed anything of any importance with me. I just knew when he was leaving and to where. But, most of the time I didn't even know with whom he was meeting. He was never gone more than a few days at a time. So, the trips just weren't that big of a deal."

"What other trips did he generally take? I mean, to what cities?"

"Well, his most routine trips were to Chicago, Dallas, and Seattle. I remember a few times over the years he went to Phoenix. But I don't remember any names of the companies or people that he met with. Ben, are you implying or thinking that Henry was involved in something illegal?"

"No, I have no indications nor have I heard anyone else say that he was involved in anything like that. But since he was doing business with a company under investigation by the FBI and he was killed on an airplane owned by that company; he and his company will be thoroughly reviewed. Have any officials been to your house yet?"

"Yes! They had a search warrant and took a lot of his business stuff; mainly his computer and files."

"Were you interviewed?"

"No, will I be?"

"I'm not sure, but that would be a normal investigative action, if they did. It wouldn't necessarily mean that they think that you have had any involvement with the company's business. But I'm sure that they will want to know what you know. So just be truthful with them and you should be just fine. Do you have any ongoing involvement with the company, now that Henry is gone?"

"No. The company's lead attorney informed me that upon the death of the CEO, a cash settlement is made which ends the beneficiary's claim or claims on the company. I received that cash settlement a few days ago."

"Oh, one other thing, did you ever go on any business trips with Henry, or entertainment that might have been paid for by one of his clients?"

"No, his business wasn't set up like that. They never involved the spouse. And if there was some special trip or out-of-town meeting, he would take his assistant; who was also his mistress."

"Ok, sorry. I guess you will just have to wait for the officials to contact you, if they feel the need."

"Well, to hell with all that!" she took his hand and said, "I don't want to talk about it anymore. I want to talk about us."

He smiled and responded with a light squeeze of her hand.

"How about you coming over to my place tonight? We can have some wine and dinner and listen to some wonderful, relaxing music."

"That sounds wonderful! I'll be there around 9:00 p.m., after I take care of Tula and get her settled in."

"No, you must bring Tula with you—and her bed!"

"Well, who in their right mind could refuse such an invitation?" he replied, with a big smile and a twinkle in his eyes.

"Ok, it's settled. I'll see you and Tula tonight for a sleepover."

"That makes my day!" He kissed her firmly on the lips.

They finished their breakfast and left. Ben was going to the grocery store and Patricia was going to JoAnn's for a short visit and to pick up Michelle.

CHAPTER TWENTY-FOUR

At 8:00 p.m., Ben showered, then packed a few things in a small bag. He went downstairs and fed Tula then placed her things into another small bag. They were off to an enjoyable evening with Patricia, arriving there just before 9:00 p.m.

Patricia opened the door and they kissed fully, then went into the kitchen. She poured some wine and checked the dinner on the stove. She was making some Chicken Alfredo, so she had to stir it until it was ready to be taken from the skillet.

He took some wine and they touched glasses and she said with a big smile, "To a wonderful evening."

"I'll drink to that!"

While she was serving the dinner, he picked out some beautiful soft jazz.

They ate, laughed, and had lots of small talk. It was a wonderful time spent together.

After dinner they cleaned up the kitchen and settled on the couch to continue their conversation; had more wine, and he opened another bottle.

They kissed more and were softly feeling each other, enjoying the time together.

Around 11:00 p.m., she said, "How about we take this to the bedroom?"

"What? Great idea!"

After a few more kisses, they got up and went upstairs.

Michelle was already tucked away and Tula had already found her bed in the bedroom. Patricia went into the bathroom for a quick shower and Ben slid into the bed.

In a short while she came out of the bathroom with nothing on but a big, beautiful smile. She leaned against the doorframe and looked at him lying in bed.

He thought, *Wow! What a beautiful woman!*

He took a good look at her full body, smiled, and said, "So, you *are* a true redhead!"

With a slight laugh, she said, "I *am*!"

"You need to come closer."

She walked over to the bed and pulled back the sheet, exposing his lean, muscular body. He had nothing on.

He pulled her close and kissed her softly on the lips. She then kissed him on the chest a couple of times as she straddled him and begin kissing him on the face and lips. She leaned backward with a soft moan.

The night's pleasure was steamy and satisfying.

They fell asleep, cuddled together as one.

At 7:00 a.m., Ben's phone alarm went off. He rolled over, but he was in bed alone.

He looked over to check on Tula, and she was gone too.

So, he got up and took a quick shower, then got dressed, and went to the kitchen where he could already smell coffee and food. As he entered the kitchen Tula ran over to him. He picked her up, kissed her, and held her for a minute then placed her back on the floor.

He walked over to Patricia and put his arms around her and kissed her, holding her close. They smiled at each other and she said, "Thanks for a wonderful sleepover!"

He slid his hand inside the front of her robe and rubbed her beautiful body. "The pleasure was all mine!" She laughed softly.

Ben turned around and walked over to Michelle who was ignoring them and eating cereal. He kissed her on the head and said, "Good morning, sweetie."

"Good morning." She was busy with her tablet game.

Ben had coffee and sat at the table where a newspaper was already unfolded. He started thumbing through it when Patricia came up behind him and put her arms around him and kissed him on the back of the neck. She held that position for a while before moving to a chair of her own.

Ben looked at her and smiled, thinking, *She really is a great gal, but I'm afraid there might be some rocky times ahead.*

"Have you made any plans about your future? Will you be staying here?"

"Well, I really don't know. My dad wants me to move to New York and work with him in his firm, and my mother, of course, wants to be close to her granddaughter. But I really haven't made a decision yet. What do you think I should do?"

"Wow, well, I'm greedy, and therefore, I would want you close to me. But I know it might be rough being in the place where you lost your husband. So, I supposd it will depend on how you are emotionally."

"Yeah, I just have to think it through and try to consider what's most important. Ben, you know that I love you. But, I'm not exactly sure how you feel about me, and about having another family."

"That, too, is complicated. Before I become too obligated, I have to see this case to an end. It's very dangerous and will be taking up most of my time over the next few months at least. Maybe even well beyond that time frame."

"I know, and I have to take that in consideration too."

They sat quietly for a while pretending to read the paper.

Finally, she asked, "Do you love me, Ben?"

"I do. I have a great deal of strong affection for you. But, as I said, the situation could get very complicated for an unknown period of time. And, during that time I will be mostly out of town. So, advancing our relationship in the near future is questionable."

"So, you think that I should move to New York?"

"I didn't say that. That has to be your decision based on your feelings and what's best for you and Michelle. But no matter where you are, I will keep in close contact with you. Because, I care about you and do not want to lose you."

She didn't speak for a while.

"Well, that makes my decision a little easier."

He didn't ask any more questions and she had nothing more to say.

It was almost 9:30 a.m., and Patricia said, "I have to get Michelle to preschool."

"Ok, I'll get my stuff ready to go."

They both got ready and left at the same time; him and Tula to his house and her to preschool. As she was driving to the preschool, she decided that her best decision would be to go back to New York for a while.

That afternoon she called her mom and gave her the news, and she immediately received a call from her dad. He was extremely happy.

CHAPTER TWENTY-FIVE

Ben called Florence in Phoenix to discuss Title One before he left for Chicago.

Florence gave him some general information about their finance picture and how much was flowing back to the Island Distribution account in the Cayman National Bank.

"Ben, I have a name of interest that we have not been able to connect directly with Title One. That person is Jesus Angelo. Angelo shows up on the staff of Morgan Development Inc. in Atlanta. It might be beneficial for you to look into Angelo before leaving Atlanta.

"I remember his name. Jesus Angelo is identified as the Investor Coordinator for Henry's company. I'll check him out. I'll also stop by Arthur Morgan's house first and visit with him. He is the new CEO/President and the brother of the late Henry Morgan. I have met him and maybe we can have an unofficial discussion about Title One and Jesus.

"Sounds great."

Ben called Arthur's house and JoAnn answered, "Hello."

"Hi, this is Ben, Ben Berkshire, Patricia's friend."

"Of course. How are you, Ben?"

"I'm fine, I was hoping to speak with Arthur, is he in?"

"No, he's at work."

"I'm going out of town in a couple of days and was hoping that I might visit with him before I leave. Do you think he would mind if I stopped over later this evening?"

"I'm sure it would be fine. I'll let him know that you would like to visit. How about around 9:00 p.m.? He should be home by then. And if he can't make it home by then, I'll call you."

"Great, thanks for your help, JoAnn."

"No problem. Talk with you soon."

Ben arrived at the Morgan's house a few minutes early and rang the doorbell. Arthur came to the door. He was very friendly and welcomed Ben into the house and they settled in the den.

They talked a little about the crash and the information about Henry's unusual death and situation. Ben explained his involvement with the case, but nothing classified.

JoAnn brought in some wine and cheese and crackers, but she didn't stay.

Ben asked Arthur, "Do you know any of the people at Title One in Chicago?"

No, not really. Henry was our primary contact with all companies that we did business with outside of Atlanta."

"Anyone else in your company work with Title One?"

"Yes, Jesus Angelo, our Investor Coordinator and, sometimes Henry would take his assistant, Ms. Bridget Monet with them. No one else, that I'm aware of."

"Did you ever meet any of the Title One people?"

"No, the out-of-state investors never came to Atlanta. Henry always went to them."

"Ok, thanks. I really appreciate you being forthcoming. I believe that you are unaware of some serious and complicated business between your company and these out-of-town investors."

"Since Henry's death, I haven't had the time to get into the books. But the strange circumstances associated with Henry's death leads me to believe that he might have been involved with some illegal business. But, before I can get anyone outside involved, I have to get more knowledgeable myself."

"Sounds like the right approach. And if I can be of any help, just call me." Ben handed him his business card.

Arthur looked at the card and said, "Investigating business, huh?"

"Yeah, and this case has become very dangerous and challenging."

"I'm aware of the problem that you had at your house. You were lucky to get out of that alive!"

"You are so right! Look, Arthur, I don't think that it would be advisable for you to mention any involvement with me, especially to folks at your company. We don't know how deep the insiders go yet."

"I agree. And I will privately start an in-house investigation of my own."

"Good idea. And I'll hopefully have more information when I return from Chicago." He turned to leave, then stopped. "One more thing—did Ms. Monet spend much time in Chicago?"

"She was on most of the trips. Henry never went up there alone. He either had Jesus or Bridget with him. Or both."

"So, we would have to assume that whatever was or is going on between the two companies, she would be fully aware."

Arthur agreed. "I think that's a good assumption."

"Could you get me a copy of the personnel files for Jesus and Bridget?"

"Sure, I'll get them tomorrow. Just come by here tomorrow evening."

"Ok, I believe that might be helpful in our investigation. I will be passing them on to my contact in the FBI. Also, I will give a copy to the AG's office in Arizona where this case is being managed."

They shook hands and Ben said, "Please say goodbye to JoAnn for me."

"I will."

Ben left the Morgan's feeling that he had made some progress into the connection between the Morgan Investment Company and Title One. He called Florence and shared what he knew and told her that he would be sending the personnel records overnight the next day.

He got home late, but took Tula for a short walk so she could do her business and then fed her. He noticed that she wasn't walking quite the same as usual. But he contributed it to the late-night walk. She ate ok and seemed to be doing fine at home.

On Monday, Alana, Ben's assistant at the office, got all the tickets and hotel reservations made for his scheduled trip to Chicago for Wednesday.

He called Corbin's number, to leave him a message about his travel plans, but Corbin answered. "Hey! What's up?"

"Oh, hi there, Corbin, I thought you would be in bed already."

"Nah, I'm knee deep in paperwork, trying to get some reports over to Florence and Barney."

"I just wanted to let you know, I'll be leaving for Chicago day after tomorrow."

"Yeah, I know. Florence called me and told me about the info you passed on to her regarding Henry's company and his brother. Sounds like you hit a little gold. Let me know how it goes in Chicago."

"I will. You better get back to your reports, and I have a lot to do tomorrow before I leave, so we can talk later."

"Roger that!" They hung up.

The next day, Ben got up early, had coffee, and decided to take Tula to the Pet Hotel, so he would be free to prepare for his trip to Chicago. Tula was excited about taking a ride and was happy when she saw the Hotel. Ben felt good about her liking the place. He hated to leave her, but was glad there was such a place for her to stay.

Late morning, Arthur called and said that the files were ready, and he would have a service deliver them to his house by noon. JoAnn would be home, so Ben could pick them up there.

"Great, and one more favor? Would you send an overnight copy to Ms. Florence Becker in the Arizona AG's office? She will be waiting for them, and she will get them to our FBI contact."

"No problem, consider it done."

At 8:30 a.m., Ben headed to the Club to get a quick bite and relax a while before going over to Arthur's to pick up the files. He was eating pancakes when a lady slid into the seat across from him.

He looked up, it was Helen. "Hey there, gal! Long time no see."

"You too. Where the hell have you been? I've missed my golfing buddy."

They both laughed and she ordered coffee. "I'm heading out to play 9 holes; want to come?"

"I don't know, I'm pretty busy right now."

"Ah, bullshit!, Come on! It only takes a couple of hours. We can catch up and plan our next rendezvous."

He laughed, "That might be a while. I'm heading out in the morning for Chicago, and don't know when I'll be back."

"Ok then, play hard to get! But we could have a few laughs before you go and a quickie in the car."

"Ok, that sounds good—except I have to skip the quickie." They laughed. "I'll change and meet you on the putting green."

They teed off around 10:00 a.m. and finished a little after noon. They parted with a kiss and hug, and headed for the showers. Ben got dressed and left for JoAnn's house to pick up the files.

When he arrived, JoAnn met him at the door, they hugged quickly, and she invited him into the kitchen.

"Wine?"

"Sure."

He took the files and opened the one on Bridget Monet.

She has been with the company for a little over two years, coming there from California. Ben noticed with interest that her personal reference was Mr. Jesus Angelo.

He opened Mr. Angelo's file and noted that he had been with the company about six months longer than Ms. Monet. But Angelo was not from California; he was from Mexico City.

Ben called Arthur. "Hi, say, how much do you know about Angelo?"

"Not much. Our personnel matters are run by Henry's secretary, Martha Blitz. She does all the interviews of prospective employees. Then, if she is satisfied, they are introduced to Henry, for a final decision."

"Well, there is something odd about both Angelo and Monet. He is from Mexico City and he was the personal reference for Ms. Monet. And they were hired into the company within six months of each other. Maybe you could do some investigative work and check their backgrounds a little closer. See if they might have known each other in Mexico? And also, maybe you can find out if they are close friends away from the office. I've got a bad feeling about those two."

"Ok, Ben. I'll have Martha dig into their pasts. Might have a PI check out their personal lives a bit."

"Can you trust Martha?"

"Yes, she has been with us for over 15 years. She is a very reliable person."

"Ok, I'll be talking with Ms. Becker at the Arizona AG's office. I'm sure that she will catch this relationship too. But I'll bring it up, just to make sure. She has contacts in Mexico City, so maybe we can get some details from them. Do you mind if I give your name to a security field officer here in Atlanta? He works for Mr. Barney Yokem from the Arizona AG's office.

I'm sure that he will want to discuss some of this with you. His name is Corbin, no last name. All their field personnel go by code names, not their real names."

"No problem. Was he involved in the problem at your house?"

"Yes, he was in charge of the complete operation. He is an outstanding Operations guy, and is excellent at decision making under fire."

"Good to know. I will wait to hear from him."

"Ok, I'm leaving your house shortly to get ready for Chicago. I'll be leaving in the morning."

"Ok, be safe!"

Ben finished his wine with some light conversation with JoAnn regarding Patricia. She caught him up on how things were going for her in New York. Patricia had moved into an apartment in Park Avenue Estates and had enrolled Michelle in a nearby pre-school.

"Wow! Big bucks!"

Patricia is working with her dad, getting her legal feet wet. "Have you talked with Patricia since she left?"

"No, I wanted to let her get settled first, and then maybe I can make time for a visit."

"Ben, it's been a long time."

"I know, I'm working on it. I need to get going now."

They walked to the door, hugged and said their goodbyes. "Take care of yourself, Ben."

"I will, and you do the same."

"I will."

CHAPTER TWENTY-SIX

Ben arrived at O'Hare Airport in Chicago about 11:30 a.m. It was a little cool, even though it was the second week in October. The windy city was trying to live up to its name. He smiled. He actually liked Chicago. The city had great food and great music.

As he was walking toward the baggage area, his mouth dropped open! It was no other than Handyman, sitting on a bench watching the girls go by!

Handyman saw him and got up. Ben said, "What the hell are you doing here?"

"Well, good morning to you too!" Handyman said, with a big smile.

"Haven't you caught on yet? I'm your shadow until this operation gets a little bit more under control. Besides, I missed you!"

They laughed and had a light handshake.

"Well, it's great to see you. Where are you staying?"

"Same as you."

"How did you know where I was gonna stay?"

"I have a friend name Alana."

Ben laughed. "I can't even keep my private assistant away from you."

"Nope!"

"You have a baggage to pick up?"

"No, I travel light; just a long military bag."

"Ok, let me get my bag and I'll meet you out front for a cab."

"Roger."

Ben went to the baggage claim and got his bag.

They grab a cab, loaded their gear, and Ben told the driver, "Hyatt House Evanston, please."

After checking in, Ben in room 510 and Handyman in 512, they headed to the bar for a beer and to discuss the latest information each of them had about Title One.

"Did Florence or Barney update you on the two employees in Henry's company that are suspects?"

"No, I haven't heard of them yet. I've been working on the Title One side of the equation."

Ben filled him in.

"So, it appears, at this point, that Arthur isn't involved."

"Yeah, that's what I'm seeing. He is being extremely cooperative and seems to be in total darkness about the money laundering and dope movement. But, it looks like the two people that were closest to Henry, Angelo and Monet, are in pretty deep. I think that we have to assume that they were working very closely with Henry on the operation."

"I agree," Handyman said. "We found a Robert (Bobby) Diaz working at Title One. He is the Vice President of Project Funding. Florence believes that he is the go-between for Title One and Island Distribution in the

Caymans. He controls all the transfer of funds. He also seems to have direct control over the movement of money from Seattle and Phoenix to the Caymans."

Handyman continued, "Barney has had him tracked for a few weeks now and says that old Bobby is in the air every few days going to one of these places.

Barney has been working with Ms. Farmer at the Cayman National Bank on comparing the incoming of funds to Island Distribution to Bobby's trips to the various locations. They seem to track very well."

"I will ask Arthur to search for Robert Diaz's name in all the correspondences to and from Title One.

Thanks, Handyman."

They finished their beer and decided to take a little break and freshen up before an early dinner.

"I'll meet you here around 5:00 p.m."

"Roget that!" Handyman said.

Ben settled into his room and called Corbin to thank him for sending Handyman to shadow him.

Corbin laughed a little and said, "Well, someone has to take care of our Texan!"

Ben laughed too. "I'll check in with you after a couple of days." And he gave Corbin Arthur's name and phone number.

When Ben hung up, he noticed that he had a voice message waiting.

He checked it, it was from Arthur's home. He immediately returned the call.

JoAnn answered, "Hello!"

"Hi, what's up?"

"I assume that you put me down as an emergency contact at the Pet Hotel."

"Yeah, did you get a call?"

"Yes." She paused. "The director there called me and said that Tula passed away last night."

Ben did not respond. He took in a deep breath. "Did he say what happened?"

"Yes, apparently she had a stroke and they could not save her."

"Well, damn! Damn!" Ben said. "That really sucks!"

"I'm so sorry, Ben, I know how much you loved that little dog."

"Yeah. She was a wonderful sidekick; I really enjoyed having her around. I'm gonna miss her so much!"

"The director said that he needs some instructions on how to handle the remains."

"Ok, thanks, I'll call him"

"I will be telling him that she is to be cremated. Would you mind going by to pick up her ashes?"

"No, not at all."

"Thanks, JoAnn, I appreciate your help."

Ben called the director and provided authorization to cremate Tula and allow JoAnn to pick up her ashes.

Ben met Handyman at 5:00 p.m. at the bar and ordered a scotch on the rocks.

"Hmm, I've never seen you drink anything but beer."

"Yeah, I got some bad news when I checked my messages. My little dog, Tula, had a stroke at the Pet Hotel last night and didn't make it."

"Well, damn! I remember her. She was such a sweet little dog."

"Yes, she was,"

"I'm sorry for your loss, Ben. We had a K9 with our team on my last tour in Afghanistan. He was a well-trained, wonderful dog. He moved around the group as if we were all his best friend; staying close and on alert every night. We lost him to an IED. So, I know a little of how you are feeling. I know you're gonna miss her."

He tipped his beer to Ben's glass and said, "To Tula!"

"Thanks, Handyman."

They drank in silence for a while.

Then Ben said, "Well, are we ready to get some dinner?"

"Roger that!"

After dinner, they met in Ben's room to go over some strategy for their encounter with Title One.

Corbin had made arrangements with a PI company in Chicago to work with them.

The name of the company was Daniel Research. They had spies, electronic specialists, ladies of the night impersonators, and almost any other special skill needed to get the job done. The goal was to make contact with a couple of Title One employees to obtain information.

"We will track Bobby when he is in town; and place listening and video devices in as many places as possible."

"Sounds good, Ben."

The next day, they made contact with Howard Daniel, the founder of Daniel Research. He was an ex-CIA field operative and had spent several years in Russia doing spy duty.

Howard was about six feet tall, maybe fifty years old, balding a bit, and appeared to be in excellent physical condition. The wrinkles around his eyes showed his sense of humor. When he shook hands, he showed a lot of teeth. You just had to like him!

Handyman and Ben had lunch with Howard. Howard's plan was to assign two of his women agents to track and make favorable contact with a couple of the key players in Title One.

Also, Howard would send a few technicians into the offices to install phone and desk listening devices. Plus, at least five cameras with audio would be installed in conference rooms and key offices.

Ben said, "I think that we should place tracking devices on all vehicles."

Howard agreed, "Good idea."

Handyman had a list of all the officers of Title One, so they picked the top five for vehicle tracking.

The Command Center for monitoring the audio and video plus the tracking of the vehicles would be an RV bus parked in a park close to Title One's office on Elgin Road.

Ben said, "Our code words are "STONE MOUNTAIN". Use them for calling or entering the RV. I rented a Tahoe SUV with Illinois tags for Handyman and me."

They were taking a break and chatting with Howard when Handyman asked him, "How many of your people are ex-military?"

"All of them, and they all have combat experience."

"Great! We only hire the same in the south."

"Yeah, I figured that, when I read the info about your shit show in Atlanta!" They all three laughed.

"I was especially appreciative of it, since it was my personal home that was under attack."

"Really! I guess I missed that part of the story."

"So, how do we get this ball rolling?" Ben asked.

"Well, first, the ladies will make contact and feed us some points of interest. Then we will focus on those people first; listening to their phone calls, watching their meetings and tracking their vehicles."

"What happens if one of the ladies is forced into a vehicle?" Ben asked.

"They have a special emergency signal on the two-way radio and we have a tracking device in their hair; it's satellite monitored, so we can get to them pretty fast," Howard said. "And they are well trained in combat self-defense." He laughed and said, "Meaner than a bunch of badgers! A Joe on the street doesn't have a chance against them."

"Good to know," Handyman said with a smile.

"Slowly, over about three days or so, we should be able to obtain enough intel to pass on to the AG for some pickups," Ben said. "And from that point, the AG personnel will interrogate them."

Ben continued, "If it goes well, we should be able to connect some dots between here, the Caymans, Seattle, Atlanta, and Phoenix."

"Also," Handyman said, "Barney, my leader in Phoenix, is hoping to make a big distribution bust from some of this intel."

"Well," Howard said, "hopefully we can help him."

Ben asked, "What's the control plan?"

Howard said, "I was hoping that at least one of the three of us would be in the Command Center at all times.

"My guys know what to do and how to respond to unexpected combat situations, but we need someone there as the go-to guy." Howard continued, "I have two-way radios for all the Commanders; three working in the Command Center, the Field Commander, the person coordinating and providing assistance to the working ladies, and the three of us.

"The working ladies are on a secondary channel with their Field Commander. But, in case of an immediate need for help, they have access to the RV Commander's channel.

"The field technicians are on another secondary channel directly to the RV Commander. And, they too, have access to the working ladies' channel.

Howard concluded, "If need be, everyone can talk with each other. So backup is just a channel switch away. Plus, if either lady got into trouble and could not talk, all they have to do is press and release their push-to-talk button three times."

"Any more questions or concerns?" Ben asked.

"No, I think I'm good," Howard said, and Handyman said, "I'm ready."

"Ok then," Ben said, "the operation starts tomorrow at noon."

CHAPTER TWENTY-SEVEN

The operation was named STING RAY.

All of Howard's players were named for the operation.

Senior RV Commander – Shark

Field Commander – Whale

Two women agents – Woman One - Bait (Rosa); Woman Two - Tackle (Megan)

Senior Technician – Sparks

Senior Audio man – Vision

The RV and all players were in place at noon.

During the prior night, Sparks and Vision had managed to install three cameras and five listening devices in the Title One offices.

One each was in Mr. Bobby Diaz's office and conference room. The others were in various conference rooms and top officers' offices.

A tracking device was installed on Mr. Diaz's vehicle; and his cell phone had been tapped.

Around 8:00 p.m. that evening, Bait and Tackle selected an upscale bar/restaurant called Rendezvous, close to the Title One office area. It served light food, mostly seafood. The night before, they had seen several of the men from Title One enter the bar. The entrance was subtle—no maître d'—but it then opened up to a large round room with a circular bar in the center, with at least four or five bartenders.

Along the outside of the bar circle, there was a wider circle of about 20 booths. Each booth had a window and a private curtain entrance, so customers could have drinks and dinner in complete privacy.

Bait and Tackle took a seat at the bar directly across from the front entrance, so they were able to see who came in and went out. There were both plain women and beautiful ladies who were well-dressed, but showing enough cleavage to draw attention.

Before they had ordered their second drink, two well-dressed businessmen approached them. They were friendly and obviously looking for some action. The two men ordered a round of drinks and, with happy faces began to settle in with the ladies. Small talk about jobs, and where are you from? have you been around here long? kept the time moving along.

One of the men was from Title One, named Alford Rise, and the other one was not. But they seemed to know each other very well.

It was finally revealed that the second man was from Seattle. He was in town on business. He said that his name was Robert Banks, and works with Multiple Family Investing in Seattle. His company coordinates investments in apartment complexes and townhomes in Washington State and California.

Bait settled in with Mr. Rise while Tackle focused on Mr. Banks. Bait introduced herself as Rosa and said that she was in town from Texas. She and her friend, Megan, were just out looking for some fun.

She asked Rise, "What kind of work are you involved in?"

"It's boring finance stuff. Mostly record keeping but with big bucks."

"So you have a very important job!"

"No," he said, "but I do handle several investors and coordinate with three out-of-state partners."

"So, Mr. Banks is one of your out-of-state partners?"

"Yes, he is an important one."

"Are all of your out-of-state partners from Washington?"

"No, I also deal with one from Atlanta and one from Phoenix."

"Wow!" Rosa said, "You must be very important."

He blushed a little, and she put her hand on his arm and said, "You want to get a booth and have something to eat?"

"Sure."

Bait nodded at Tackle, and she and Rise walked around the bar to an open booth. He slid in and she did the same, on the same side with him; not real close, but close enough to make a statement.

Rise was obviously not a ladies' man, and he wasn't comfortable in the bar pickup environment. So Bait had control of the situation.

The waiter came over, gave them a menu, took drink orders, and closed the curtain to their booth.

Bait looked deeply at him and kissed him on the cheek. He placed his hand on her knee. She had on a short dress and his hand was warm. But he didn't attempt to become aggressive.

"So, you are in the financial department of your company?"

"Yes."

"How long have you been at Title One? That's the name, right?"

"Yes, Title One. I'm the Assistant Vice President of Financial Coordination; just a fancy name for an administrative job."

She laughed lightly and squeezed his arm a little. "I'll bet you have a lot of control over funds in that company."

"Oh, yeah, I do, but it's small compared to the funds that others manage for off-shore accounts."

"You have off-shore customers too?"

"No, not customers, but accounts where we manage the distribution of funds for out-of-country projects."

"That's way over my head! I don't really understand what you are talking about!"

She smiled at him. Rise's eyes lit up with admiration for her and he quickly kissed her on the mouth. She didn't resist, but she also didn't respond in kind.

Their drinks came and they ordered some baked oysters on the shell and fries.

As the evening went on and Rise had more to drink, he revealed that the guy he was with, Robert Banks, was the Vice President of the company in Seattle; and that they were working on a major investment project being funded by a company in Mexico City.

It was getting close to midnight, and Bait and Tackle were instructed to check in at the RV at midnight. So Bait told Rise that she had to find her girlfriend and meet some other people, but she would love to meet him for drinks some other time.

Rise's face lit up. "That would be great!"

Bait called Tackle on her cell. Tackle and Robert Banks were still in the bar too, in another booth. Tackle told him she had to go meet her friend, and left.

Bait and Tackle met out front of the bar and got a cab, rode around a few minutes to make sure that they were not being followed, then had the cab drop them off on a corner close to the RV.

They were debriefed by Shark, the RV Commander, and went to their hotel.

Whale, the Field Commander, spoke up first. "Well, I guess we have to get more information from Mr. Alford Rise. From what Bait is telling us; he might be easy to squeeze."

"Yeah," Shark said, "Bait needs to set up another date with him and see what she can find out."

Ben added, "That company that Mr. Banks works for in Seattle was identified by Florance out in Arizona. It is one of the major laundering locations. So we could also make a second run at him."

"I think you're right, "Shark said. "So, Whale, you call both of the ladies and have them set up another date with these guys."

"Ok, and while they are together, we can bug their car and get a tap on their cell phones," Whale said.

"Excellent plan," said Howard. "Let's rap this up for the night and get those dates set up."

Whale called the ladies and discussed the plan with them. They decided to get Messrs. Rise and Banks to meet at the same location, the Rendezvous, at 9:00 p.m. the next evening.

The two ladies took a cab the next night and were on time for the meeting. Both of the men were there, waiting outside. After brief kisses on the cheek, they held hands, and all four went into the bar together. It was crowded, but Mr. Rise gave the guy a big tip and they went into a booth.

Drinks were ordered and the men were obviously delighted to be with Rosa and Megan again. Small talk followed and, after a couple of drinks, the men expressed a desire to become more intimate. Mr. Banks asked for a separate booth for himself and Megan.

After the booth became private, Mr. Rise leaned over and kissed Rosa on the lips and put his arm around her. Rosa responded in an attempt to make him more relaxed and secure with her.

After a few minutes of groping, Rosa eased away from him and gave him a kiss on the cheek. She said, "Can we move a little bit slower? I'm really not used to this."

He sat up straighter and said, "Oh! I'm sorry, I didn't mean to make you feel uncomfortable."

"You didn't. I just haven't been with a man for a while. Let's have another drink." He ordered their drinks and she started a conversation. "Have you lived in Chicago very long?"

"No, I moved here from California a few years ago."

"Why did you pick Chicago?"

"Well, I was doing about the same job in California, and I was contacted by a guy that worked at Title One. They got my name from the internet and offered me over twice the money I was making out west. And I had gone through a divorce out there; so it gave me a way to start a new life."

"Tell me more about what you do, please. It sounds complicated, but so interesting."

"Oh, it's not that complicated. I record funds moved from agents in the field and then distribute those funds to our contacts in various locations in the country. They send funds back to me, then I transfer all of those funds to our holding account in the Cayman National Bank."

"So, you are an important hub of operational control for all those funds?"

"That's about it!"

"Wow! That is really an important job!"

They ordered some light dinner and he excused himself to go to the bathroom.

She called Whale, "Did you get all that?"

"Yeah, great job. It's almost midnight, so you might want to get out of there in the next half hour or so. We need to have a meeting before we close down."

"Roger."

Mr. Rise returned, they ate, and he suggested they get a room.

"Maybe next time. I have to be somewhere else with my friend before midnight. But I had a wonderful time, and I'd like to take a raincheck on the overnight."

"Yeah, ok. That would be great."

She called Tackle and they met out front and got a cab back to the RV Command. After about 30 minutes of discussion about Bait's date with

Mr. Rise, Ben said, "I think that we should pass him off to our FBI contact and see if they can scare him into working for them. He should be able to provide the account numbers, major players at several locations, and more details about Title One's operation."

Handyman said, "It doesn't appear that Mr. Rise is fully aware of the exact nature of his operation; he's just pushing papers and moving money, so he should roll pretty fast."

"Ok," Howard said, "I'll pass our recommendations on to Barney and he and Florence can take it from there."

"Great job, ladies," Howard said to Bait and Tackle. "I'll let you know if we need to make further contact with these guys. In the meantime, you can report back to the office."

The next day, Florance called her FBI contact in Arizona and passed on the details of the sting operation that was carried out in Chicago.

The FBI agent immediately reported it to the Chicago office for action.

At noon, an FBI agent in Chicago picked up Mr. Alford Rise leaving his office building for lunch, and took him back to their office for an interview. It took less than an hour to convenience Mr. Rise that he was involved in a major criminal operation and that he had to cooperate with them or possibly go to jail.

He agreed to cooperate.

A meeting was set up for the following evening at the FBI office. Mr. Rise was supposed to bring copies of all of the account information that he could find, and to make a list of every major player in all of the offices that he could find in his files.

Rise left the FBI office and took a cab back to his office.

That evening at Mr. Rise's home, he answered the door and a man shot him in the head with a 357 magnum, and walked away.

The following morning, Howard read about the incident in the paper and called Ben. "They discussed the ramification of the incident and decided that Title One must have been watching Mr. Rise when he went into the FBI office. Unfortunately, Mr. Rise was killed before the FBI could obtain the desired information.

Howard terminated the STING RAY operation, and Ben and Handyman headed back to Atlanta to regroup with Corbin.

CHAPTER TWENTY-EIGHT

Ben decided that he would take a little break from the investigation project with the AG in Arizona. He had a strong desire to see Patricia. He called Florence and Barney and discussed it with them and they felt it was probably a good idea to step back and regroup.

He called Patricia.

"Hello."

"Hi, sweetie!"

"Ben! What a wonderful surprise! Are you in town?"

"No, but I was thinking about coming up and spending a few days with you, if you aren't too busy."

"That would be great! I've missed you so much!"

"I've missed you too! How about tomorrow, is that too soon?"

"No! I can't wait! It will be wonderful seeing and kissing you!" She laughed a little, "And other things!"

"Yeah, that will be great for sure. Ok then, I'll let you know my travel schedule and when I will be arriving. What is your address?"

"I'm in the Park Avenue Estates, 500 block, Apartment 200."

"You sure they let cowboys in that place?" he chuckled.

"They better let *MY* cowboy in!" She laughed. "Oh, Ben! It will be so wonderful to hold you. Hurry!"

"Well, I'll see you tomorrow, my dear. Love you!"

"Love you too!"

They hung up

Ben called Alana and asked her to make reservations for his travel, then went over to the club for some lunch. He was eating a sandwich and fries when in walked beautiful Helen. She spotted him and broke into a big smile, walking in his direction.

"My dear Ben! How are you?" She kissed him on the cheek and gave him a big hug.

Hi, Helen, how's the old golf game?

"Not the same without you! I've missed you. Were the hell have you been?"

"Oh, in and out of town and country. Got a case that has really been kicking my ass!"

"Does it have anything to do with that war-zone-type fiasco?"

"Yeah, it sure does, and that was just part of it. And it's far from over."

"Sounds like you need a break! Have a little fun, let your hair down! You need a good roll in the hay! My place or yours?" She smiled.

"As tempting as that is—and it is—I'll have to take a rain check. I have to get packed for a trip to New York for a few days."

"Well, if you don't give me some attention soon, I'm gonna begin to think that you don't remember how great I am!"

"That just isn't possible!" They both laughed.

Helen gave him a big hug and kiss and said that she had to get to the first tee.

Ben received the itinerary from Alana, stopped by the Pro Shop for a few minutes, and then drove home.

When he pulled into his driveway, there were two men in suits standing in front of his open garage door. One was a tall black guy around 40 with wide shoulders—looked like a lineman for the Cowboys. And the other one was of average height, in his late 30's, with biceps that filled out his suit jacket sleeve.

Ben got out of his car and said, "Something I can do for you guys?"

"Yeah," the older one said as they both pulled out badges. "We have a search warrant for this house."

"Really? And what exactly are you searching for?"

The guy said, "We can't discuss that with you right now. Are you the owner, Benjamin Berkshire?"

"I am, but before you can come inside, I need to call downtown and verify the warrant."

Ben had noticed that the paper didn't have an embossing stamp on it, a requirement for a search warrant.

He walked inside and locked the door behind him. Went to his office and took out his 9mm. He heard a car start up and looked out front. The two guys had gotten into their car and were leaving.

He called 911 and reported the incident to a desk sergeant and requested a detective come to discuss the incident with him. A detective, Lt. Dannar, arrived in about half an hour. They introduced themselves to each other.

Det. Dannar said, "I was one of the responding detectives the night of your combat incident. Glad to see that you're ok. Who do you think these guys might have been?"

"Yeah, thanks, that was quite a mess, for sure. This almost *has* to be something to do with the case I'm still working on with the FBI and AG of Arizona."

Did you get a plate on the vehicle?"

"Yeah. It was a Georgia plate with the word "OFFICIAL" on it; a large black SUV, maybe a Navigator."

"Great," Detective Dannar said. "We will have a patrol car around your neighborhood for the next few days and try to catch these guys if they return."

"That would be great. I'm leaving town tomorrow for a week. So let me give you my cell number, just in case." He gave the detective the number and the detective departed.

The next morning Ben was up at 6:00 a.m., putting the final touches on his packing and notes for the housekeeper. His flight was at 11:30 a.m. from DFW International. Even though he has a badge that gives him express boarding rights, he still likes to get there an hour or so before departure.

At 9:45 a.m., his cab arrived and they drove to the airport. He was flying American out of Terminal A. After he was all checked in, he went to Dunkin' Donuts; they have great coffee.

He was sipping on his coffee when a lovely black lady came up and sat down beside him. She was well-dressed, and had on expensive-looking jewelry. She definitely was not a hooker.

He looked at her and said, "Well, good morning." She smiled and said, "Good morning to you, Mr. Berkshire."

Ben leaned back and looked at her more closely. "Have we met?"

"No, my name is Becky Wondergrass. We have some common, shall we say, friends?"

"Hum, and who might they be?"

"Handyman and his crew. I've been assigned to keep an eye on you. You know, make sure you don't get into trouble." She smiled.

Ben smiled. "Well, you are definitely an upgrade from any other member of Handyman's crew that I've met so far."

"Well, thanks, I'll see you when we land." With that, Becky got up and walked away. Ben thought, *A beautiful sight!*

He immediately called Handyman and they chatted a few minutes. Handyman confirmed that Becky was one of his team and was very capable of taking care of herself and supporting him, should there be any trouble in New York. Ben thanked him and they hung up.

During the flight, Ben had the opportunity to visit with Becky for a while. Turns out, she was more than qualified to provide support for his well-being.

Becky was 33 years old and had been with Handyman for little over five years. Her initial training was with the FBI special tactical team, with assignments in several combat zones. Her more recent training has been provided by two former Navy Seals who worked with Handyman.

Becky wasn't married and loved her job! She was from a little town in Georgia, Waycross, and was a graduate of Georgia Tech, as an engineer.

She was funny, and spending time with her was a real joy. Ben was most impressed!

The flight went fast and upon arrival Becky gave him a special two-way satellite radio so they could have immediate communication, one on one.

They were walking out to Baggage and Ben said, "I better give you the address where I'll be staying and the person's name."

Becky gave a light laugh and patted him on the cheek. "Ah, sweetie, I know all about you and Patricia and where you are going. You just have a great time and I'll be around. Remember, you have no worries with ol' Becky watching you! This isn't my first rodeo!"

He laughed and thanked her. She left him at Baggage and disappeared.

He grabbed his bag and departed the terminal to wait for Patricia.

He didn't have to wait long; she came flying up in a beautiful light-blue Mercedes convertible. She jumped out of the car and into his arms, with her legs wrapped around his waist! She couldn't stop kissing him. It was a great reunion!

CHAPTER TWENTY-NINE

For a week Ben and Patricia had a wonderful time. Patricia set up a couple of parties to introduce Ben to her New York crowd. They all enjoyed meeting the real cowboy from Texas; someone who had such an exciting life.

And, of course, Patricia had already shared with them the war zone incident that occurred at Ben's house and the masterful way in which Ben and his team had handled it. Her friends had also read all the gory details in the New York Times as it had unfolded. So now to meet the actual person! Great!

They all had many questions about the "intra-workings" of such a dangerous and exciting operation. Ben was patient and forthcoming with them because they were Patricia's friends, but he didn't get into any confidential details.

They spent time at the theater and some wonderful restaurants. Ben especially enjoyed a small place in Manhattan called Ellen's Stardust Diner located on Broadway and 51st, in the Theater District. It had a 1950s theme and wonderful food and service.

At night, they would slide in between the expensive silk sheets and have wonderful, loving, intimate times. Patricia just could not get enough of him. Nor he, of her!

Times to remember!

Ben was up early, a cup of delicious coffee in one hand and the New York Times in the other, reading about the many interesting activities of the night. Something that was never ending in the Big Apple.

A story about a young Marine caught his eye.

The marine had been arrested because he had defended the rights of a lady on a subway. According to the story, the young marine had given up his seat for an older lady, and some hoodlum had quickly taken the seat. When the guy was asked to get out of the seat, he pulled a knife and the marine took it away from him; a fight broke out, with the marine getting the better of the hoodlum.

The hoodlum received a broken jaw and damaged knee. Several of the onlookers told the NYPD officer that the marine started the fight. So, he was arrested. The marine was from out of town, visiting the Big Apple for the first time.

For Ben, it was disturbing, because of his own military background. He wanted to look into the case and see if he could help. Ben laid his paper down and begin to think about being an active lawyer again. Taking a sip of his coffee, he wondered just how hard it would be to activate his license in New York. He would have to discuss the matter with Mr. Hampton, Patricia's father.

While he was mulling over the possible change in his life, Patricia entered the kitchen. Her lovely and exciting smile filled the room.

"Good morning, sunshine," he said, as she wrapped herself around him and gave him a loving kiss.

"Good morning to you, too!"

She picked up a cup and went over to the coffee pot. "See anything exciting in the paper?"

"Lots of routine political and criminal stories. About what you would expect in a city of millions. Say, what would be a good time to visit with your dad? I have something that I would like to get his opinion on—a personal matter."

"Do you want to run it by me? Maybe I could help."

"Well, not quite yet, but I will, after I have discussed it with your dad."

"Ok, I'll give him a call and see when he would be available. What would you like to do today? It's gonna be a beautiful sunshiny day, my love."

It was 10:00 a.m. by the time they had showered and dressed. Patricia dialed her dad's office.

"Good morning, Maggie, is Dad in yet?"

Maggie had been with Mr. Hampton for many years and had known Patricia since she was a little girl.

"Good morning, Patricia, how are you today? And yes, he is here."

"Great, may I speak with him?"

"Sure, just a moment, please."

Mr. Hampton came on the line. "Good morning, dear."

"Good morning, Dad. I hope everything is going well. I don't plan to come in today; Ben and I are going to run around town and maybe have a late lunch."

"Everything is under control; you two have fun."

"Dad, Ben has a personal matter he would like to discuss with you, when you have time."

"Of course. Tell him to come by around 3:00 p.m. today and have a cup of coffee with me."

"Great, Dad, thanks. I'll tell him." And with a little chuckle she said, "Have a great day, and stay out of trouble."

He laughed. "You know me, 'Mr. Nice Guy!' Love you!" They hung up.

She found Ben in the study, looking over some law books. "What are you up to?"

"Oh, just perusing this impressive law library you and your dad have."

"Yeah, it is impressive. He has been collecting law books from all over the world for decades. All of the states are here and major cities in other countries. Actually, it is enjoyable just to sit and read in here at times."

"I suppose you could get lost in the many stories of so many case studies. I used to really enjoy practicing law."

"Well, maybe you should try it again. I'm sure glad that I have come back to work with my dad."

"Yeah, maybe I should."

"Oh, by the way, Dad said that three this afternoon would be a good time to drop by, if you want to."

"Yeah, that sounds great. Let's plan on that."

At a quarter of three, Patricia and Ben arrived at the law office. Patricia went to her office, and Ben stopped by the reception area to chat with Maggie. He had not formally met her, but had had several conversations with her when calling Patricia from Texas.

"I believe that Mr. Hampton is available now," Maggie said, as she got up and rounded her desk to show Ben to Mr. Hampton's office.

Patricia's Dad was pleased to see Ben, and they had a hardy handshake.

"Good afternoon, Mr. Hampton. I appreciate you making the time to see me on such short notice."

"Oh, my! Feel free to drop by anytime. And, please, call me Charles. I hope you are enjoying your stay in our fair city."

"Yes, absolutely. I have a wonderful tour guide!" Ben smiled.

"That you do! Well, Ben, what is this personal matter that you would like to discuss?"

"I have been thinking about becoming active in practicing law again. And as you know, I'm sure, I have been focusing on my investigative business, and in doing so, I have been involved in some very dangerous situations. I believe that it would be more enjoyable to practice law than to chase bad guys all over the country."

"I can see where that would be a good decision on your part, if you love the law."

"I do. And, I wanted to get your input on a couple of ideas. First, I would like to have some idea about just how long it might take to activate my Texas license in New York. And, second, if you might have a spot in your firm for me."

"Well," Charles said, with a smile, "that's a lot of thinking on your part. The answer to your first question is, I believe that I could pull some strings and get your license activated within 30 days. When you became involved with Patricia, we did look into your work as a lawyer in Texas, and we were impressed. You were primarily involved with criminal law, is that correct?"

"Yes sir, that's correct."

"Well, we have no shortage of those cases. So, Ben, I would be very pleased to have you as a part of our criminal division—if Patricia doesn't have a problem with it. You know that her happiness is of the utmost importance to me."

"Of course. I planned on discussing it with her, if you had any interest."

"Well then, let me get Maggie started on the paperwork to the Bar for the activation of your license, and then we will discuss finances and position."

"Sounds great! I will look forward to hearing from Maggie. And thanks, Charles, I'm sure that it will be a good match. And, by the way, there was a story in the paper today about a young out-of-town marine who was arrested for giving up his seat for a lady on a subway. Something about a hoodlum grabbing the seat before the lady could sit down. There was a fight and the hoodlum got the worst of the deal. Several bystanders said that the marine was at fault. Is that a case that your firm could look into?"

"Is it important to you, Ben?"

"Yes sir. I hate to see military personnel get mistreated, and he is in the city all alone; 21 years old and just trying to do the right and honorable thing."

"I'll have someone take a look at it."

"Thanks, Charles, I really appreciate it."

They shook hands.

"Have a good day," Ben said.

"You too."

Ben went to Patricia's office. She was deep into the review of some case.

He reached over and kissed her on the back of the neck. She turned around and leaned back to receive a loving full kiss from him. It was a different kind of kiss; she could feel it. Something that seemed to carry with it a special meaning.

After the kiss, she stood up and put her arms around his neck, kissing him back with equal intensity.

Then she said "Ok, what's going on?"

"Well, the bottom line is, you have to make a decision if you want me full time or part time."

"What? Exactly what does that mean?"

"I have discussed the possibility of me becoming a member of this firm with your dad, and he is leaving it up to you."

Patricia jumped up and down laughing, with tears coming into her eyes.

"OH MY GOSH! Are you kidding? REALLY?"

"Yes, really."

"Your dad says that it would take around 30 days to get my license activated in New York and that he would be pleased to have me in his criminal division. But he wanted to make sure that you were ok with it."

"Ben, that is so wonderful! I just can't believe that you want to come to New York and work as a lawyer."

"I do not want to spend the rest of my life chasing bad guys all over the world. And I love you, so coming to New York and working with you and your dad just seems to make sense."

"Oh! I love you so, so much Ben! We will have a wonderful life together. I am so very happy right now!"

Ben spent the next couple of weeks talking with Handyman and the other folks that he had been working with as an investigator, making sure that all the loose ends were closed.

He went home to Atlanta to made arrangements to move his household goods to New York and to close his Atlanta office.

He kept Alana on as an assistant for a while, until everything was closed and she had found a suitable position with another business.

Then he took his last trip from Atlanta to New York . . . ready to begin his new life with Patricia and as a criminal lawyer in the Big Apple.

The ending . . . and a new beginning!

Acknowledgements

I have had several people proofread and check this manuscript over the last three years. I am very grateful for their help.

I want to thank my daughter Robin, who provided recommendations on plot, names of characters and other parts of the story. She also proofread the complete manuscript several times.

I want to especially thank Mason Bell. She has been the pillar upon which the book has been build.

Her continued review and recommendations have provided me with great insight.

About the Author

Charles Hood has been involved in education and writing for over 45 years. His teaching included advanced engineering classes in the military and the University of Hawaii. He also taught satellite communication classes at the University of Houston.

He spent 20 years in the U.S. Navy with four tours in Vietnam from 1962 to 1968. After his wife of over 45 years, Shirin, passed away, he wrote his first book, "Why Me", a memoir.

He is currently working on a three-book series based on the character Benjamin Berkshire. Mr. Hood has lived in The Woodlands, Texas for over 45 years.